I0575990

GRIGGS
TOWN

GRIGGS TOWN

C.L. SELLORS

To my sweet Lora

My brother, Cecil, and I have spent our whole lives on this miserable patch of earth in southwest Virginia, known as Colby Valley, a place no one seems to visit and no one dares to leave. The population around here is only 3,253 people, according to the sign at the town's entrance, and I don't expect the number to change anytime soon.

And you might find it hard to believe, but in all my years of living here, I've never gotten to engage in an official conversation with anyone who was born and raised outside Colby Valley. Now don't get me wrong. I've definitely engaged in a little small talk with a few outsiders who were simply passing through, such as the occasional traveler searching for a gas station or the random truck driver delivering goods to Mr. Jenny's store—a store that sells everything from barbed wire to chicken eggs—but not once have I ever had a genuine conversation with any of them.

I've tried my best to get stories from them about the outside world and how things are out there compared with here, but they always act like they are in too big a hurry to talk to me. Sometimes they seem amused by how slow I talk, as well as my country accent, and they will often ask me to repeat words I've just said because they want to hear me say them again, but other times they want to talk only about how nice or how bad the weather is while they walk away from me to get back to their cars.

I would love to know more about the outside world, but nobody wants to have that conversation with me. I've even tried to ask my own family what it's like, but most of them either act like they don't know or say that there is nothing worth talking about. I used to believe them when I was younger, but now that I'm getting older, I am starting to think that they don't want me to know because they're afraid that I'll leave this place if I get to hearing too much.

But thankfully, I met a kind old man named Mr. Drewey earlier this year. He was filling up the newspaper rack at the gas station and offered Cecil and me a free newspaper, so I'm starting to hear and read a lot more about the outside world. Mr. Drewey is the owner, journalist, and editor in chief at *The Colby Times* (a one-man operation). He's a real talker who loves to tell a story, and unlike everyone else around here, he doesn't seem to get the least bit aggravated whenever I ask him questions. In fact, he acts like he enjoys it.

Some of the places he's been telling me about are even better than I could have imagined, but one place, which sits about seventy miles to the west of us, is more appealing than them all. A place that sounds too good to be true. A place called Griggs Town. Mr. Drewey tells me that Griggs Town has been buying advertisements in his newspaper since 1983 and that if it wasn't for them buying all those ads for the last few years, he couldn't pay the bills. Of course, Mr. Drewey won't tell us how much money the folks in Griggs are paying him to place the ads, but it must be a fair amount because he always delights in handing us a free newspaper.

Ever since Cecil and I got to know Mr. Drewey, we have made the same morning trip down to his printing shop to get our free newspaper, hoping to hear more about this Griggs Town place and hoping to one day find ourselves a job there. These morning trips have been going on for about five months now, and the routine is always about the same. He slides the newspaper toward us in secret, as if he doesn't want anybody to know that he's handing it out for free, and then we rush away to the old barn on our family's farm to read it. Cecil always climbs up on the tractor, sits down, and talks nonsense while I sit on the ground and scan through the paper. To start things off, I read interesting headlines and joke about there never being any local help wanted ads, but what I look forward to the most is reading about Griggs Town.

The articles about Griggs Town are always inviting; they make it sound like the most desirable place in the world. Numerous articles describe how respectful and hospitable the people are. And to hear them tell it, there isn't one person in Griggs Town who wouldn't give you the shirt off their back if you asked for it. The articles make it sound like this place would be more comfortable than home, and they never fail to mention that everyone is welcome there.

The Colby Times also has several pieces of writing about the "might" of the Griggs Town economy. These articles contain a lot of technical language, so they can be a bit difficult to understand, but the parts that do make sense are interesting. They make every guarantee—almost saying that they swear on their lives—that Griggs Town is one of the most prosperous places in the world. They also go as far as claiming that "all levels of business and industry have grown at such a rapid rate that the local workforce is not large enough to sustain their growth." The big problem with that claim is that every job they've been seeking help for requires a lifetime of previous experience.

Every help wanted ad that comes from Griggs Town reads "experience required," "knowledge preferred," or "only experienced applicants need apply." Every time I open one of Mr. Drewey's hot-off-the-press newspapers, I hope to find an ad lacking those restrictive words, but every ad shares the same stomach-kicking conclusion. Our work experience doesn't surpass digging in the dirt and shoveling manure on the family farm, and right now that doesn't qualify us to do anything. It's discouraging at times, but we keep looking and hoping that we will find something soon. If we are lucky, maybe there will be something new in tomorrow morning's newspaper.

2

The next day, Cecil wakes up before me and kicks the top bunk, the little space where I sleep, and wakes me. These are the same bunk beds that we've slept in since we were kids. They held us well until our preteen years, but now that we're getting older, they're more like short wooden hammocks, where limited parts of our bodies find room to rest in comfort. A real bed would be nice, but the small bedroom we share doesn't have enough space. "Wake up, Greenway," he says, kicking the underside of my bunk bed.

"I'm awake, and you can stop kicking," I say. And yes, my name is Greenway. It sounds more like a grassy area along the side of a rural highway, but somehow I've been stuck with this name since birth. I check the clock and see that it's just 5:30 a.m. This is strange because Cecil never gets out of bed before nine and I'm often the one waking him. "Why are you up so early?" I ask.

"Well, I don't know. I woke up and couldn't get back to sleep. But it's sort of strange. The first thing that popped into my mind, soon as I opened my eyes, was that Griggs Town place. Maybe it means something. Let's go get the paper."

"It's too early," I say. "Mr. Drewey's probably still sleeping. And there's no telling when he'll have the paper ready. He's an old man, and he doesn't get in no hurry. I've never seen him delivering the paper before noon."

"Yeah, but I just can't wait. Let's go down there and see if the lights are on. He might be an old man, but I say he's already up and working on it. He won't mind."

I've lived with Cecil long enough to know that when he gets his mind set on something, the chances are slim that you'll be able to convince him otherwise, so I give in and agree. We sneak through the house, careful not to wake anyone, then we slip out the back door and take off into the darkness, feeling our way through a path that we've never traveled without the sunlight by our side. A half mile later, we find ourselves staring at Drewey's printing shop, not just the home of *The Colby Times*, but also the home of Old Man Drewey.

"I see light," Cecil says. "I had a feeling he'd be up. Let's go." Cecil takes off running toward the dim light, a single light glowing through one of the building's narrow windows. I follow at half the pace, unsure how Mr. Drewey will welcome us at this time of day.

Instead of a gentle knock in the darkness, Cecil warms up the front door with the style of an angry woodpecker.

"What's the matter?" Mr. Drewey asks, pulling the door open with caution, face creasing with worry.

"Nothing's wrong," Cecil says.

Mr. Drewey pushes his ink-smudged eyeglasses higher on his nose and studies us. "You sure you're all right?"

"Yeah, we're fine," Cecil assures him. "I know it's early; I tried to tell him it was. But Greenway said you would have the paper ready by now—said he couldn't wait—that was him banging your door down." Cecil deals me a secret grin, privately bragging for placing the blame on me.

Mr. Drewey takes a sip from his coffee cup, licks the black fluid from his snarled white mustache, and focuses his attention on me. "Well, what's the hurry? It isn't even daylight out there yet."

"No real hurry," I say, sensing it's too late and pointless to try to shift the blame.

Mr. Drewey glances down at his loosely banded wristwatch, squinting through his glasses to make out the numbers. "Seems to me like you're in a hurry. I've never seen you two come knocking on the door this early in the morning." He swings the door open and steps away from the entrance. "I haven't even prepped the press for printing yet. But it won't take long. You two are welcome to come on in and wait."

I've always wondered what it looks like inside Mr. Drewey's printing shop, so after receiving a genuine invitation to enter, I begin to forgive Cecil for pinning his alarming woodpecker knock on me. We follow him through a plywood-lined hallway, where old front-page newsprint hangs in a generic fashion behind dusty panes of framed glass, and he leads us into a room constructed of the same aged plywood material. Along the wall sits a row of blue wooden chairs that look like they haven't been sat in since before I was born, while tables holding stacks of old newspapers line another wall. In the corner of the room, a thin door, supported by a pair of rusty hinges, is tied open with a web of butcher's twine.

"Pick out a chair and follow me," Mr. Drewey says as he leads us through the tied-open door and stops us a few feet inside a shadowy room where a faint beam of light from the adjoining room breaks up the darkness. "It will be fine if you sit here," he says. The slight echo of his voice bounces back from the room's distant walls and repeats itself in my ears. "Make yourselves comfortable. I already have the printing plates ready; it won't take me but a few minutes."

Mr. Drewey drags his squeaky sneakers to the corner of the shop and yanks the chains on three different lights dangling over his printing press to turn them on. We watch as he straightens a stack of oversized papers and places it on top of the press. He circles the press, inspects the various mechanisms, punches a hole in a can of ink, and pours it into a shallow tray. With the side of his hand, he smacks a short lever and powers up the press. Metal wheels chatter and shake as the prehistoric creature comes to life, spitting dust and dried ink into the air. Mr. Drewey steps up onto a short stool and feeds the sheets of paper through a series of shiny steel rollers. And after a little while, the printing press spits a knee-high stack of folded newspapers onto the floor. He disconnects the power to the press, grabs a newspaper from the stack, and says, "Follow me to the other room; the light is better in there."

Abandoning our blue chairs, we follow him through another doorway and stand next to him beside a table cluttered with stacks of dusty newspapers. We watch in silence as he unfolds the fresh one he brought with him and examines it with a steady eye and a magnifying glass. "Looks pretty good," he mumbles. He reveals a warm smile, refolds the newspaper, and tosses it to us. "Here you are."

With great eagerness, I open the paper and start scanning the ink-scented pages.

Mr. Drewey continues. "I know you two have been faithful when it comes to reading the Griggs classifieds, but how serious are you about leaving Colby Valley? Over the years, I've heard lots of people talk about leaving, but at the end of the day, nobody ever follows through with it."

"Yeah, why wouldn't we leave?" Cecil barks. "There isn't anything here for us. We're pretty much grown men, and I'm about sick of living in that old house with everybody, especially our lazy cousins. I ain't figured yet why everybody thinks Colby's so doggone great."

I break into the conversation, trying to soften Cecil's tone, sensing that Mr. Drewey doesn't appreciate all his fussing. "We just figure on leaving because there is nothing here for us. You know that, Mr. Drewey. We've been searching for work nonstop since we finished school, but nobody is ever hiring around here; and if they are hiring, they won't hire us. And we're tired of being broke. In all our lives I don't reckon we've ever had more than five dollars to our name."

"Well, I suppose that's about as serious as you can get," he says. He strokes one eyebrow with his fingers and purses his lips as if deep in thought. "And I guess I can't blame you if you do. Though I suppose your folks would be against you two leaving, wouldn't they? It's sort of a tradition around here for the kids to take over the family farm, isn't it?"

"I know they won't like us leaving," I say. "But I can't see living at home and piddling around on the farm for the rest of my life. And as far as tradition goes, I want no part of it. That farm never put a dime in my pocket."

"Never put one in mine, either," Cecil growls. "And I don't see how it ever will."

"Well," Mr. Drewey says slowly, still seeming deep in thought, "you know as well as I do that they're mostly looking for skilled workers in Griggs, but I think if you two are patient and keep watching, something will come together sooner or later."

Mr. Drewey grabs a pencil and begins scribbling on the corner of an old newspaper as Cecil elevates his voice in frustration.

"I guess that means there ain't anything new in the paper today, huh? You could've told us that before going through all the trouble of printing the paper and all this talking."

I shoot Cecil a look, trying to get him to tone down his voice, but he doesn't seem to be taking the hint. He opens his mouth like he's about to say something, and I hurry to interrupt. "It's all right, Cecil. It won't help matters any by you getting all bent out of shape."

I am worried that Cecil has ruined our friendship and our free newspaper privileges with Mr. Drewey. But Mr. Drewey tears the corner off the newspaper that he has been scribbling on and, with more grace than I would expect, says, "I know it's frustrating. I've been around long enough to know what it's like when things don't work out the way you want them to. But listen, I've been doing some thinking, and I might have an idea, maybe even a remedy to your problem."

"A remedy? What kind of thinking? What do you mean?" I ask.

"Well, I started thinking, since you all are that serious and since I think you two are pretty good young fellas, I could make a few phone calls to Griggs Town and see about finding you all a job. I can ask around and see if there are any other jobs that they're not sending me. But you've got to promise me that you won't mention this to your folks. I think they would get awful upset with me if they found out I had anything to do with you two leaving Colby Valley."

Cecil looks at Mr. Drewey and smiles. "You're kidding us?"

Mr. Drewey grins while staring at the little piece of paper in his hand. "Come on now, Cecil. You all have been coming to see me for—what—about five or six months now? Have you ever known me to kid around?"

"Well, I reckon not," Cecil admits. "But then again, this is about the most talking we've ever had the chance to do with you. But if you're being for real, I won't say a word to our folks. Will you, Greenway?"

"Of course not. I will take any job they offer me. I'll do whatever it takes to get me out of Colby Valley. Please just tell them that we'll do whatever. But do you think you know somebody who will hire us, even without experience?"

"Well, I don't know, Greenway, but I got a couple of ideas I've come up with here. I need to make a few phone calls to some of my clients to see what they have. No guarantees that they will put you to work, but I'll give it my best shot."

"Are you going to call them now?" Cecil asks, eyes stretching wide. He turns his ear toward Mr. Drewey as if he may have to listen closely for a response.

"I can't go ringing their phones right now," Mr. Drewey explains. "It's only about half past six, and I suppose I had better wait until everyone in Griggs Town gets to work and gets settled in." He pauses, looks at his little piece of paper again, and says, "But listen, that's not all I was thinking. I was also thinking about a little something else. I'll wait till about nine or so before I make the phone calls, but in the meantime, I was thinking that maybe you two wouldn't mind helping me out with a few chores around here. You can take care of a few things that I've been wanting to do but are hard on an old man like me."

"I'll help you do whatever, just as long as you make that call," Cecil says. He straightens up from his slouched position, parks his foot on the edge of the table, and begins tightening his shoelaces. "What do you got? What do you want me to do? Do you want me to stack up these here papers on the table?" He swaps feet, as if his legs were bolts of lightning, and tightens the laces on his other shoe. "Well, do you?"

Mr. Drewey chuckles and says, "Just give me a minute, and I'll show you." He takes off toward the door and leads us back into the printing shop. Then he hands us each a broom and a dustpan. "This is what you can do. You two can take your brooms and sweep this room out. And please be sure you reach under the furniture and the printing press and pull all the dirt out. Then as soon as you are done sweeping the floor, you can grab an oilcan, dab a little oil on the rags—the ones over there on the shelf—and wipe down the printing press the best you can. And while you are at it, wipe anything else that looks like it could use it. Just take your time and be careful. That ought to keep you all busy until about nine. I'll make some calls then."

Cecil pouts at the sight of a broom but agrees that a broom is a decent trade-off for Mr. Drewey's promise to help us find a job.

Cecil and I start swinging our brooms across the floor, releasing a plume of dust into the air. The floor must have been holding on to all that dust for several years. After about an hour of careful sweeping, I think we manage to get about half of the dirt into the dustpan and the other half of the dirt redistributed throughout the printing shop and onto the walls, the furniture, and the printing press. But nonetheless, we did get the floor to look pretty good. And as it turns out, there was some shiny oak flooring under all that dirt. I think Mr. Drewey will be pleased.

Finally, we're happy to set our brooms aside, grab some rags and a can of oil, and make our way over to the printing press. As we are discussing who gets to tackle which part of the large machine with the oil, Mr. Drewey shouts for us. We look up at the dusty clock and see that it's not even eight o'clock yet, but we rush to the other room and find Drewey with the phone at his ear. He smiles when he sees us and tells the person he is speaking with to hold on for a minute. He covers the phone receiver with one hand and speaks to us in a low tone. "I'm sorry, but there may be a change of plans. I don't think I am going to be able to call my clients in Griggs Town at nine like I planned." He pauses for a second, watching us as if to gauge our reaction, and says, "Or shall I say, I might not need to call them."

Cecil and I stare at each other, confused, as Mr. Drewey beams with excitement and continues his phone conversation. "Thank you for holding, Mr. Slusher. That was them that just came into the room. If you like, I can put them on the phone for you." And after a short pause in which he appears to be listening carefully, Mr. Drewey covers the phone receiver once again with his hand and says, "Listen here. A gentleman from Griggs Town is on the phone, and I think he will put you to work. As luck would have it, he just called me, wanting to place an ad. He started talking about experience, but when I told him about you two and how honest and hardworking you are, he said he could use honesty more than anything and that he would like to have a word with you. Which one of you wants the phone?"

"You take it," Cecil demands, looking at me. "You're better at talking to people."

And before I can even respond, Mr. Drewey hands me the telephone.

"Hello," I say.

"Hi, there; the name is Bodie Slusher. Drewey tells me he's got two fine men who are eager to work."

"Why, yes, sir, we've been looking for work," I say, noticing that the nervous jitter that started in my stomach when I grabbed the phone has somehow made its way to my voice.

"All right, now tell me what you would think about working at the Swift silver mine in Griggs Town. It might not always be easy—it could be hard labor sometimes. But do you think you would be up for it? And are you dependable?"

"Absolutely. Yes, sir. I'm more than up for it, and I'm dependable too."

"Now, what about the other guy? Mr. Drewey said he is your brother?"

"Yes, sir, he is my brother, and he wants to work just as much as I do. We both need it. We love working."

The phone goes silent for a moment, and all I could think was that I can't believe that I just told the man that we love working. What was I thinking? That sounded like such a stupid thing to say. That made me sound like a little kid. I brace myself for the worst as his voice returns to the phone.

"That sounds good," he says. "Now, how soon can you start? Can you be ready to go right away?"

"Well, we got to do some things before we can leave here, but I think we could make it in a few days, maybe sooner."

"All right. If you two can be here and ready to go in a few days, you can consider yourselves hired."

"Are you sure about this? Is it guaranteed?"

"Yes, it's guaranteed. I usually don't hire a man over the phone, but Mr. Drewey spoke right highly of you two. I need a few honest, hardworking, and dependable young men."

"Well, we won't let you down, Mr. Slusher."

"I'm sure you won't. Now please give me your legal names. I will start on all the paperwork and put you on the list."

"My name is Greenway Pochaw, and my brother's name is Cecil."

"Okay, guys, I'll be seeing you soon. There is a guard booth at the entrance of the mine. Just ask for Mr. Slusher when you arrive. And please tell Mr. Drewey I said thanks."

"I sure will, and Cecil and I will be there soon."

As soon as I hang up the phone, Cecil starts in on me. "What did he say? It sounds like we got a job, don't we?"

"Yeah, Cecil, I guess so. I asked him if he was sure, and he said it's guaranteed. But there is just one problem: we're going to have to find a way to get there soon. He said be there in a few days, and we're hired."

Cecil walks over, places his hand on my shoulder, and squeezes. "Thank you, brother. Good job. I knew you could talk to him." This is strange behavior for Cecil. He has never been one to express appreciation or give me credit for anything. And besides, I managed to get just a few words in with Mr. Slusher. But based on Cecil's shifting facial expressions, the appreciation appears to be leaving him already. "Wait a minute," Cecil grumbles. "What kind of work is it, and what does it pay?"

My heart sinks a little on the second part of his question. "He said we would be working at the Swift silver mine, but I didn't think to ask him about the pay—guess I got too excited and forgot all about it."

As Cecil opens his mouth to speak, I brace myself for his disgruntled groans, but the tone of his voice is more pleasant than I expected. "I suppose that will be fair enough," he says. "No matter how much it pays, it will sure be better than what we're making now, which couldn't be closer to nothing." He squeezes my shoulder again and says, "I reckon we better get going. We have a lot to do in a short amount of time and a long way to go."

Cecil and I say our goodbyes to Mr. Drewey and offer him our best expressions of gratitude as he guides us to the front door.

"Wait a minute," Mr. Drewey says, rolling his arm to motion us back. "I almost forgot." He reaches into his back pants pocket and pulls out a faded brown leather wallet. "This is for you, and this is for you," he says, handing each of us a crisp twenty-dollar bill.

"What? Are you serious? What is this for?" I ask, squeezing the bill between my fingers, staring at it, and taking in the promising scent of it.

Mr. Drewey smiles and says, "You didn't think I would ask you to help me out around here for nothing, did you? You boys did a fine job on that floor in the printing shop. Now take this money and get what you need to make it to Griggs Town. And whatever you do, please don't tell anybody that I gave you that money. Because if you do, I'll have half of Colby beating on my door and looking for work. And please don't mention to your folks that I helped you get a job, either."

"I won't say a word about it," I say, almost telling him that he didn't have to pay us for helping, but not willing to suggest that he should take the money back.

"I won't say a word, either," Cecil says.

"I'll assume that's a promise. Now, I got something else for you too." He pulls a sheet of paper from his pocket and hands it to me. "Here. Since you've never been out of Colby Valley, you're going to need this map to find your way. It's hand drawn, but it should be simple enough to follow." Mr. Drewey takes a step back, smiles, and says, "Now, get out of here and get yourselves to work. You've got a good seventy-mile journey ahead of you."

As soon as Mr. Drewey shuts the door, Cecil dances across the front porch and says, "I just can't believe it, Greenway. We got a whole forty dollars. We don't even need to go to Griggs Town now." He grins and looks back over his shoulder at me as he runs off. I cannot tell if he's being serious or not.

"What, are you crazy? You think forty dollars is enough to stay home and forget about Griggs Town? You can't be serious."

"Sure it is. We're pretty much rich now, wouldn't you say? I've never had this much money before, and it'll take forever to spend it. Maybe we can just take it and start our own business or something here in Colby Valley."

"Well, yeah," I respond, trying to catch up and keep the pace as he takes off, running back toward our house. "Forty dollars is a lot of money, but I'd say it would be easier to spend than you think. You can have your twenty, but I'm going to take mine and head to Griggs Town. The money we have now is nothing compared to what we can make there."

"Do you believe we'll make more than that?"

"Like I said, I don't know what silver mining pays, but I think we'll have hundreds in our pockets instead of twenties. And you seem to forget that this is what we wanted—to get away from Colby, giving us a chance to make it on our own, giving us a change in life. Plus, it will get you out of the house and give us a shot of making something of ourselves—that's what you want, isn't it?"

Cecil slows down and waits for me to catch up with him as we get to where we can see our family's farm. Out of breath, red-faced, and panting, he looks at me and says, "Ha, Greenway! You know I'm just messing with you." He smacks me in the back of the head, takes off running again, and says, "Stop screwing around and get moving. We got a long way to go, and we need to get packing."

Since we don't own any suitcases, we decide to stop by the barn and grab a couple of empty feed bags. The bags are constructed of woven plastic, and although empty, they still hold that distinct smell that only a pig would love. Stamped across the front of the bags are the words PIG FEED in five-inch-tall blue letters. We won't look fashionable carrying these silly things around, but I guess they will have to do the job.

We walk through the door at home, and our dad and Uncle Tibbs and a few of the cousins gather around to question us over the feed bags. And as soon as we mention that we'll be packing our belongings in them, the room floods with laughter. Our mom and Auntie Rose come rushing in from the kitchen to observe the commotion. Moments later, we are also joined by Grandpa and the rest of the cousins. The laughter rises to a boil, but then the room falls silent when we explain that it's no joke and that we will be leaving at once and going to Griggs Town. They are all standing around with their arms crossed, and the look on their faces suggests that they're waiting for us to put the joke to rest.

But Cecil and I assure them that this is no joke—that we did get a job and that we will be leaving. Mom and Auntie Rose begin sobbing while the rest of them chime in with their disapproval.

"There ain't no way you two boys are going to make it," Uncle Tibbs shouts. He is the motor mouth of the family, who always races to be the first to slip his words in where they don't belong. It is his specialty. "You boys don't know the first thing about responsibilities; you don't know jack crap."

"I'm about sick of hearing you talk, Tibbs," Cecil says, almost puking his words, his face flushing red with anger. "I'm a grown man, a grown man who knows more than you ever thought."

"Grown man, my rear end," Uncle Tibbs says. "Grown men don't live at home with their mommies."

"Well, that sure is a funny thing for *you* to say," Cecil says. His face is getting redder, and the look in his eyes warns that he could charge at Uncle Tibbs at any second. "The last time I checked, you're living at home with my mommy too. The whole family lives here, all because ain't nobody got a drop of money and can't afford anything else. But unlike you, we're leaving, and I don't see your butt having plans of going anywhere."

"You better watch your mouth, boy. You mark my words, you'll never make it out there—you'll get eaten alive—come running back home like a pup with his tail between his legs."

I try to join the argument, but Grandpa butts in before I can speak. "Tibbs is right; you boys know nothing—don't know even half of what you think you do. You are just boys. That's all you are, just boys." He kneels, pokes his pipe stem into his shoe to scratch the side of his foot, and continues. "You're setting yourselves up for disaster. Things won't be any better where you're going, like you think. Why do you reckon I have never left Colby Valley? I've been here my whole life, for good reason."

I make a second attempt to join the argument, but then the rest of the family starts in on us. They are all going at it at once, and I can barely pick a word or two out of anything they are saying. I never expected all this fuss. You would think that most folks would be glad to see you better yourself, but that doesn't seem to be the case when it comes to my family. If they would settle down for a second and let us try to explain, then maybe they would see our side of things.

Mom leaves the room for a second and returns with a soup pot and a wooden spoon. She holds the pot up high and strikes it good a few times with the side of the spoon. *Clang—clang—clang.* "If you all don't knock it off and let them talk, I won't be cooking anyone supper tonight," she threatens.

"And I won't bother helping, either," Auntie Rose adds.

Mom scours the room with her wrathful eyes and declares, "You better be giving my boys a chance to speak, whether you agree with them or not. And I mean it." After Mom's warning, silence fills the room long enough to allow us to speak. "You go first, Cecil," she orders.

Cecil crosses his arms and grits his teeth. "You go ahead, Greenway. I don't have anything else to say to them. I just want to get my things packed and leave. I'll show them that I can make it, and I'll make it much better than they ever thought about making it." A short burst of laughter breaks out as Dad and Uncle Tibbs compete to be the first to break Mom's code of silence. Dad wins.

"Daggone it, son. I don't know who it is you all think you are fooling, there isn't any work out there. You won't find anything outside this farm, and you'd better come to terms with it."

"Sorry, Dad," I say. "But it's a little too late for you to try to tell us that now, we already have a job waiting on us. All we have to do is show up and claim it—"

"Sure, you do," Uncle Tibbs says. "You two ain't got a brain between you. Somebody done promised you the world, and now you two done gone and believed it. You don't have a job. You got an imagination is what you got."

Mom strikes the soup pot again. *Clang! Clang!* "I told you all to hush it, and I mean it."

Cecil takes off to the bedroom. "I'll be packing my things!" he shouts as he slams the bedroom door. Another round of laughter breaks out as Dad and Uncle Tibbs attempt to finish sharing their wisdom with me, but Mom cuts them off short this time with the wooden spoon and the soup pot.

"Don't bother with it, Mom," I say. "It is nothing but a joke to them, but I can promise you this, they are going to find out just how wrong they are about us. They're going to see! I'll be with Cecil packing my things." Laughter erupts once again as I take off down the hallway.

Cecil and I pack what few clothes we have, as well as other things we think we may need, into our feed bags. Mom and Auntie Rose come into the room and try to apologize on behalf of the rest of the family. "They aren't sorry about anything," Cecil says. "I can still hear them laughing down the hallway."

"Mom," I say, "it's not your fault. There's no need for you to be sorry because of them. It's not your fault, either, Rose. As soon as Cecil and I get our stuff together, we'll be out of here."

"I don't want my boys to go. I'll be sick if you two leave," Mom cries. Auntie Rose nods her head in agreement, suggesting that she will somehow also be sick.

"I'm sorry, but we, for once in our lives, have to do what is best for us," I say. "And what happens to be best for us is getting away from this farm." A tear rolls from Mom's face and falls to the floor, requiring me to think fast and offer some comforting words. "Don't cry, Mom. It's not like we're going to be gone forever, just long enough to make some good money. When we get there, you and Auntie Rose will never have to worry about money again. We'll send you some as soon as we get it coming in."

Mom dries her face with her shirtsleeve. "How far away is it, and how do you two plan on getting there? And how do you plan on eating? And where will you sleep?"

Cecil jumps in. "Well, I thought I was going to ask for a ride from Dad or Tibbs, but I am not asking crap from anybody in this house, and at this point I wouldn't take a ride even if they begged me. I doubt anybody's car would make it anyway."

"It doesn't matter," I say. "We will make it somehow. It's just seventy miles from here. Not that far."

"You and Auntie Rose could come and see us when we get settled, you know," Cecil adds.

"Well," Mom says, the tears now showing the first signs of slowing. "I guess it ain't right for me to try to hold you boys back when all you want to do is make a better life for yourselves." She sniffs and smiles and uses her shirtsleeve again to dry a final tear. "You didn't answer me, though, when I asked you where you'll eat or sleep. Do you have a place to stay when you get there—somebody who will feed you?"

"I don't know," I say. "Cecil and I have forty dollars between us, and I suppose that will get us all we need. It should take care of us until we get our first pay."

The sadness in Mom's face unravels into an expressionless stare. "Forty dollars! Where did you get that kind of money?"

"Relax, Mom," I say, realizing that it will be hard for her to understand how we are able to possess such a large sum of money. "It's honest pay. We just happened to get a little lucky with an odd job, that's all."

Mom pauses for a minute while appearing to bounce my response around in her head. She crosses her arms, looks at me with interrogating eyes, and says, "No, really. How did you get it? Do you mean that somebody had work for you here in Colby Valley?"

"Yeah. Is it that hard to believe?" I ask, knowing that it is but not willing to admit it.

"I'd say so. Forty dollars is an awful lot of money. And I haven't heard of anybody in Colby Valley paying out that kind of money for just an odd job. Most people take care of their own work around here and don't hire it out."

"Well, it's true. He ain't lying," Cecil says.

"Who gave you the work, then?"

"There's no use in asking," Cecil says. "We ain't supposed to tell."

"Why is that? I'm your mother." The "I'm your mother" bit is Mom's first line of offense whenever she receives any resistance from me and Cecil. The bit never works, but she still uses it.

"I don't know why. And that doesn't matter. But we ain't supposed to tell," Cecil says, as he deals her a squinty-eyed look. Mom stares him down as he shuts his mouth and tightens his lips in front of her, an expression that suggests any more attempts at prying will be useless.

Mom looks at me once again for answers, assuming I might break. "Who gave you work and the money, Greenway?"

"Sorry, Mom. I can't say. If we tell, he said that half the people in Colby Valley will be beating on his door and looking for work, and he said he doesn't want that. We made a promise, so there is no use in prying. And I'm not going back on my promise. But I don't see why it matters anyway."

Mom shakes her head, acknowledging her failed attempt at prying, and stares us down with disappointment. "Okay," she says, hinting that she is eager to change the subject. "You boys promise me that you'll be careful and write me when you get there."

And after being forced to swear that we won't "wind up getting hurt or dead," we say our goodbyes to Mom and Auntie Rose, grab our feed bags, and sneak out the back door to avoid the rest of the family. We then head to Mr. Jenny's store to buy some food for the journey.

Mr. Jenny is one of the rudest old men I've ever known, and he is the last person that I even want to talk to, but no one else in Colby Valley sells what we need. I hope we can get in and out of there without a fight.

We stash our bags in the drainage ditch beside the store while trying to dodge the nosy stares of the old men loitering in career-like fashion next to the store's entry doors. The same men, it seems, that I can remember loitering there since I was old enough to walk.

We rush through the store trying to get everything we think we might need and decide that four cans of potted meat, a box of saltine crackers, two big Granny Smith apples, and a gallon jug of water will be enough to make it to Griggs Town. We figure that we don't want to carry any more than we have to and can stop at a store along the way if we need anything else.

Mr. Jenny is working at the cash register when we go to pay for the food. He tilts his head back and stares down at us, looking smug as a cat with a bowl of cream, before keying the prices of our food into the machine. "That'll be five dollars and thirty cents," he says, extending his open hand. I reach into my pocket, hand him the crisp twenty-dollar bill, and his mouth drops open in disbelief. "Where did you boys get this kind of money?"

"We got it from working," I say.

The folks standing behind us in line start snickering, priming Mr. Jenny to do the same. "I'll bet you got it from working," he says, making extra effort to display his doubt. "I've never seen you boys or any of your folks come in here to buy anything without holding up the line and counting out change to pay for it." He winks at the customers in line behind us and pauses for another laugh.

"Is that so?" Cecil charges, pushing his shoulders back, cheeks flushing red with anger. "You're trying to say we're good for nothing but holding up the line and counting change, are you? If you want to act like that, it won't be anything for us to take our money elsewhere and spend it."

"Oh, no need for that," Mr. Jenny says. He stretches his wrinkled lips to display a nasty grin as he eyes the twenty I gave him. "I'm just picking with you boys. But the last time I checked, there's no other place in Colby Valley to buy food. You might as well spend it here."

"Bull crap," Cecil spews, the red in his cheeks now spreading into the skin of his forehead. "You can buy live chickens and eggs all day long and as many as you want, down the street, right in front of Dorsey's place."

"Mr. Dorsey couldn't make change on a dollar," Mr. Jenny mumbles. "And you'd have to spend the whole twenty to walk away with anything." He hurries to secure the twenty in the cash drawer and then hands me the change. And with the twenty no longer in danger of being withdrawn, he drawls, "Your folks must be doing pretty good if they can afford to pay you that kind of money for working on that wasted farm."

I have always tried to respect my elders, but this old man here is putting me to the test. "Whose farm around here isn't wasted?" I say. "Besides, what's it to you? Cecil and I just come in here to buy a few things, and all you want to do is put my family down and treat us all like bums. You don't have the right to go mouthing off like you do."

Mr. Jenny tries to speak, but I won't let him get a word in. "My folks are doing the best they can do—just like everyone else. What's it to you if they have to scrape together change to pay? It keeps you in business, doesn't it?"

"Um . . . um . . . well, I'm sorry," Mr. Jenny says without an ounce of sincerity detectable anywhere in his voice. "I just ain't never seen you boys buy this much before and have more than enough to pay for it. What are you boys going to do with all that potted meat? Are you having a family picnic or a wedding or something? I'll bet somebody's getting married, aren't they?"

"Ain't nobody doing all of that with only four cans of potted meat, and you know it," Cecil barks. He turns around to cast a mean stare at everyone standing in line behind us, then turns back to face Mr. Jenny. "It's just one awful smart remark after another from you, isn't it? But even though it's none of your business, we bought it because we're leaving this stupid town."

"Sure you are," Mr. Jenny says, about half choked with laughter. "Nobody leaves Colby Valley."

"Laugh all you want, but we'll be out of here before the day is over with," Cecil growls as he yanks a plastic bag from beside the register and starts bagging our food. I turn around and notice that everyone in the store, even the old men who were loitering out front, have gathered around to watch.

"You two bums are the old pig farmer's boys, aren't you?" the tall and slender man standing in line behind us says with a laugh. I've seen him no fewer than a dozen times, but I can't remember his name. For my own personal enjoyment, I'll refer to him from here on out as "the jerk." After all, he is acting like one.

Cecil and I ignore the jerk, but Mr. Jenny takes it upon himself to give an answer. "Yep, those two are Ben Pochaw's youngins," he grunts.

"That's what I figured," the jerk says, spilling enough arrogance that you can almost smell it. "They aren't going anywhere; they are going to be like the rest of them Pochaws—sorry as a sack of crap and good for nothing."

Cecil turns around, stares the jerk dead in the eye, and says, "You listen here, stupid—"

I grab Cecil's arm, realizing that he is seconds away from dealing the jerk a cold fist. "Come on, Cecil," I plead, knowing that one little fight could get us in enough trouble to keep us from getting to Griggs Town. "Let's just please get out of here. These people aren't worth it."

Cecil appears to think about it for a second, but he agrees. "All right. You're right, Greenway, we'll go. We've done spent too much time already talking to these idiots." Unable to fight the temptation, he turns once again, this time stepping toward the jerk, and says, "That's right, I said 'idiot.' And if you know what's best for you, you won't open up that soon-to-be-busted mouth of yours again about my folks."

I grab Cecil's arm again. "Come on, man. Don't worry about it. Let's go. We've got better things to do, as if you don't remember."

"All right, but let me get one more thing." Cecil turns back around and points to the shelf behind Mr. Jenny. "I'll take the best pouch of cigarette tobacco and rolling papers that you got. And while you're at it, you might as well give me a handful of them free matches."

Mr. Jenny shoves a pouch of tobacco, papers, and a stingy handful of matches into a plastic bag and drops it on the counter and stabs the buttons on the register with his finger. "That'll be three dollars even."

Cecil grins as he reaches into his pocket and pulls out his twenty-dollar bill to pay for it. Mr. Jenny mumbles, "They got another twenty." He shakes his head in disbelief, fumbles through the cash register drawer, and hands Cecil his change. And without speaking another word, Cecil and I exit the store and rush down to the drainage ditch to fetch our bags.

We crouch down in the ditch to stay out of sight as we pack the food into our bags. "That was some good thinking back there," I say.

"What's that?" Cecil asks, as the red in his face begins to fade.

"Buying that tobacco just to show him that we had more money. That was on purpose, wasn't it?"

Cecil looks at me and grins, his face now back to its natural shade. "Yeah, that Mr. Jenny's eyes about sailed from his head when I pulled out that other twenty. I hated to waste the three dollars, but I had to show everybody that we had another twenty."

"That serves him right," I say. "I thought for a second that he wasn't going to have enough money on hand to make change."

"Yeah, me too. I'll bet you it's burning them up. They think we're loaded, and you know they'll be spending the rest of the day trying to figure out how." We swap a few smiles, a few chuckles, take a quick look at the hand-drawn map, and start walking. "You know what, Greenway? I don't think I've ever heard you go off on anybody as bad as you went off on Mr. Jenny back there. It's sort of nice to see you stand up for yourself—saves me from having to do it." He laughs, smacks me on the back of the head, and runs off a little ways ahead of me. Then he stops. "I can't run too far," he says, panting as he drops his bag on the ground and sits on it. "This bag's too heavy to be doing all that. I'm just picking with you, Greenway."

I don't say a word. I figure if I do, it will only invite him to pick at me even more, and we'll be into it with each other before we even make it out of Colby Valley. He waits until I catch up with him. "You know what gets me mad the most?" Cecil asks.

"What's that?"

"The way Mr. Jenny was running off at the mouth about our folks having to dig for change just to pay; that makes me so mad."

"I know what you mean. It makes no sense that he talks that way about our folks just because they don't have much. He won't know what to think when we start making some money and sending it home to Mom. She'll be able to go into that store and buy whatever she wants, and it will tear him up just as bad as it did when he seen all the money we showed him."

"Yeah, but I hope that when the family sees how good we're making it, they will just say to heck with Colby Valley and move to Griggs Town with us. I say they won't be able to resist when they start seeing all that money."

"I hope you're right. But all this talk has me feeling not so good about things, and I wish we could do something about it now. You know, we have plenty of money, and I was thinking that we should take some of it and give it to Mom and Auntie Rose before we go. I don't feel right about having all this money when they have none."

"Well, if you want to, that will be all right by me," Cecil says. "You know, the more I think about it, that sounds like a wonderful idea. That'll even twist Mr. Jenny's panties in a bunch that much more—that is, if we can talk them into spending it at his store. He will think we've all done got rich or something. Let's go ahead and give them a twenty; the rest will be enough to last us."

"We'll have to give them smaller bills," I say. "We already broke those two twenties."

"Yeah, but Mr. Jenny will think that it's just the change that he gave us, so let's stop somewhere and put our money together and trade it for another twenty."

I give the rest of my money to Cecil, a total of fourteen dollars and seventy cents, and we stop by the post office and trade to get a twenty and rush back home. From the edge of the yard, we can hear Dad and Uncle Tibbs inside the house rambling on about something, and we are reminded why we were in such a hurry to leave home in the first place. And without much debate, we agree that going inside is a terrible idea. We want to give Mom and Auntie Rose the money, but we don't want to go back in there and go through all that fussing again. After a little thought, we come up with what seems to be a good enough idea: we will hide the money in a steel tube in the barn, and when we get to Griggs, we'll send out a letter and let them know where it's hidden. I wish we could give it to them right now, but I guess this will be better than nothing.

Cecil and I hide the money and take another quick look at the map. Without even looking back, we toss the feed bags over our shoulders and head off—in what we hope is the right direction—to Griggs Town. After about an hour's worth of walking, we appear from beneath a canopy of trees and approach a freshly paved two-lane highway, a place that we have never seen before.

5

"Let me see the map. I think we're supposed to turn right here," Cecil says, as he impatiently rips the map from my hand before I can even extend my arm to release it to him. He unfolds the map, examines it, and says, "That's what I thought. We need to take a right, right here." Cecil turns, takes a few steps, drops his feed bag on the side of the road, and sits down on top of it. "We ought to hitch a ride. There isn't much point in wearing ourselves out with a bunch more walking. I'm going to sit right here and rest my legs until a car comes by."

"Why are you doing this?" I say, trying to suppress this severe feeling of aggravation that is boiling up inside me. "We need to keep walking, and then when we see a car, we can start thumbing for a ride. We have a long way to go, and we don't have time to just be sitting here and waiting for a car. I haven't seen a car since we started walking today."

"Forget that, Greenway. There's no point in wearing ourselves out walking if we don't have to. Let's just use our brains for once and sit here and wait for a few minutes."

"But Mr. Slusher is figuring on us being at work in a few days. I told him we would. And who knows when we'll even see a car? We can't afford to wait."

"Come on, Greenway, relax a little. We have plenty of time. This road here is about as fine as any road, and nobody would have gone to the trouble of making it good and smooth if nobody ever drives it. I'll bet a lot of cars travel this road."

I drop my feed bag and sit down beside him. This is a ridiculous idea, but I know that Cecil's impatient nature won't let it go on for too long. As I expected, after about thirty minutes of sitting in the same spot and not seeing the first car pass, Cecil finally stands up and motions me to start walking. "Well, I guess everybody's still sleeping in this morning."

He immediately starts walking, and we step off alongside this unfamiliar stretch of highway. It's only springtime, but the sun is bright and scorching. And with the heat radiating from the pavement, it feels like it is more than a hundred degrees out here. A cool breeze or a long row of shade trees sure would be pleasant.

After a few hours of dragging along this blistering road, we see the first car come up behind us. I hope it's one of those air-conditioned cars I've read about. Cecil motions for me to drop my bag and prepare myself.

"You better stick your thumb out now; we don't want to take any chance of them missing us," he demands. And as requested, I stand by the side of the road and poke my thumb out. It looks like it might take another minute or two for the car to arrive, so I don't see the rush in doing this already, but that is just his way of thinking.

The car approaches. It's a newer model that is sure to have climate control. The driver slows down, looks us dead in the eye, waves his hand, smiles with chilly lips, and keeps driving. "That selfish idiot," Cecil shouts. Honestly, I feel like saying the same thing, but I suppose Cecil said it with enough conviction for both of us. And once Cecil's facial expressions finish throwing a temper tantrum, he says, "I can't believe folks act that way. If I were driving, I'd be glad to help out a man who needed a ride."

And to my surprise, just a few minutes pass before we spot another car heading in our direction. And once again, we stand with our thumbs prematurely poked out. As it gets closer, I can see that it is a beat-up old rag of a car. It looks like it has been wrecked a few times too many: the front grill is broken out, the bumper is hanging loose on one side, and the rest of the body appears to be made up with a variety of incompatible junkyard parts. I doubt it has air-conditioning. It sounds like a barrel of nails skipping down the highway, and the closer it gets, the more I get the feeling that I should put my thumb away. The driver slows the car a little as he approaches, but he doesn't stop. I feel relieved that it's passing as Cecil shouts, even louder than the time before, "Keep on driving, you selfish idiot!"

Cecil and I toss our bags over our shoulders and start walking again. And when we come around a small curve, we see that old rag of a car has stopped and is idling on the shoulder of the road. The engine roars up and down, as the exhaust rattles and hiccups. "Good grief," I say. "He must have heard you yelling at him. I'll bet he's aiming to cause us some trouble. You have to stop blowing up at people like that."

"Who cares? I ain't worried about that idiot. I'll tell him what I said to his face."

Apparently, the man in the car sees us, so he eases back out onto the road and guns the car in reverse. The car's transmission whines like a fevered and congested piglet. My stomach begins to twist itself into a knot as Cecil drops his bag to the ground and says, "You just stand back. I'll take care of him." When the car gets next to us, it stops sharply and produces a short skid. My stomach knots up the rest of the way as a slender man with sharp cheekbones, long stringy black hair, and pale white eyeballs leans over and pops open the passenger door. With the door open, I see he's wearing black denim jeans and a stained white T-shirt. There is a moment of silence as Cecil and the driver quietly stare each other down. I prepare for the worst as the driver opens his mouth to speak.

"You boys trying to hitch a ride?" the man asks in a broken, phlegm-filled rasp.

"Yeah, we've been trying," Cecil says, surprisingly unfazed by the "boy" label.

"Where are you trying to make it to?"

"Griggs Town."

"Ahhh, yes, I know all about Griggs Town. I'm thinking of stopping there myself. I will give you a ride if you can come up with some gas money. I'm down in the red already, and with you two and all the extra load, it'll burn it out that much faster." I don't like the looks of this guy, so I am hoping that the driver's request for gas money will be enough to make Cecil refuse the offer.

"Well, how much gas money is it going to take?" Cecil asks suspiciously.

"That depends on how much you got; the more the better. This car drinks the gas."

"Well, in that case, we don't got that much."

"All right, how does five dollars sound? Can you at least do that much? I'm sure you know by now that don't many cars travel this stretch of highway."

"I suppose I can do five, but that'll about break us. Couldn't you do less?"

"Less wouldn't budge the needle. We need to make it five, or I'll have to go on without you."

"I guess it's a deal, then. Guess we ain't got no choice."

"Let's see the money. You're going to have to let me have it beforehand...so I know you got it."

Cecil counts out five dollars to the strange man, gives me a relieved look, then smiles and says, "All right, we got us a ride." He hands me his feed bag. "Put this in the back with you." Cecil hurries to grab the front seat, as if he'll beat me to it, oblivious to the fact that I've been standing in silent protest. I don't want to enter the heap, front or back. The driver of the car looks impatiently at me out of the corner of his eye and fans his foot on the gas pedal to keep the engine from dying.

"Well, are you getting in or what?" he asks. I don't know what to do. All I know is that I have no desire to get into this car; just thinking about it is making me anxious.

I consider letting them go on without me, but Cecil joins the driver's impatient stare, increasing the pressure on me, and blurts, "Come on, Greenway. Get your hind end in here."

I want to tell him no, but I guess I don't have a choice, considering we have a job waiting for us in Griggs Town. Reluctantly, I give into the pressure, toss in our bags, and climb into the back seat of the old heap.

I reach out to shut the door, but I lose my grip on the door handle as the driver stomps on the gas pedal. He darts out into the road and speeds off down the highway. The door flops back and forth as I grab the headrest on the front seat, trying to hold on and not get sucked out of the car. Fortunately, the door swings with enough momentum to shut and latch on its own.

The car's engine roars and knocks as the scent of exhaust fumes rises through the rusted-out floorboard, filling our noses with carbon monoxide. I crack the window for air and dig through the random bits of clothing and the empty snack wrappers that occupy the back seat to locate the seat belt, thinking that if I can at least find that, it will offer me a little bit of security, but there isn't one. Perhaps it has fallen through the crack in the seat. I consider reaching my hand through the crack to find it, but the benefits of finding it don't seem to outweigh the risk of what my hand may encounter. From the looks of this car, I imagine at least a few rats live in there.

"The name is S," the driver says.

Cecil looks at the man oddly. "Your name is what?"

"My name is S."

"S? Like the letter? Like the alphabet?" Cecil asks.

"Yes, that's what they call me, and that's what I like to be called. It doesn't mean anything, so don't ask. Figure it best to get that out of the way first." He adjusts the yellowed rearview mirror and looks at me. "What are your names?"

"Well, they call me Cecil, and my brother's name here is Greenway."

"Greenway? Now, that's a funny name."

Cecil kicks around the mountain of empty Vienna sausage cans on the floorboard to make more room for his feet. And the man, who now apparently goes by one of the twenty-six letters in the English alphabet, says, "Bet y'all thought I wasn't going to stop for y'all back there, didn't you? The truth is, I heard one of y'all calling me an idiot back up the road, and I take that it wasn't Greenway back here, since he doesn't talk."

"Yeah, that was me," Cecil admits without an ounce of fear or hesitation in his voice—he seems proud to admit it. "I figured you weren't going to stop and—well, it peed me off. But nothing personal. We were burning up out there walking. It feels like it's a hundred degrees out there."

S applies more pressure to the gas pedal, increasing the roar of the engine and the rotation of the car's bald tires. He smirks at me through the rearview mirror before returning one eye to the road and one eye to Cecil. "It ain't no big deal," he says. "I tried to stop the moment I seen ya, but these brakes are like sponges. You can't stop when you want to. I got to use the emergency brake to slow her down. She'll stop fast when she's going slow, but if I get her going over thirty, they ain't no such thing as stopping on a dime. But most of the time, she'll putter on down to a stop if you yank the emergency brake."

It's not enough that he has been driving like a maniac since we got into the car, but now I have to worry about whether or not he can even get the brakes to work when we need to stop. What if somebody pulls out in front of us? What if we come upon a curve that is too sharp? We will be lucky if we don't get in a wreck and die before we even make it to Griggs Town.

I see a sign on the edge of the road that reads speed limit 40, so I lean forward to take a glimpse at the speedometer to see how fast we're going, but I can't see anything through the car's grime-covered instrument panel.

"What are you looking for?" S asks.

"I was just trying to see how fast you were going."

"Would you look at that! The green boy does talk. What—are you skeered or something?"

"Well, it seems to me that if the brakes don't work, that maybe you ought to not be going so fast."

"I ain't going but fifty-seven."

"But the sign back there said the speed limit is forty miles per hour."

S laughs and applies more pressure to the gas pedal. I hope Cecil will jump in and support me in the conversation, but he doesn't seem to be the least bit concerned about all the reckless driving. In fact, he appears to be having fun with it. I guess he and S are both crazy, and I'm the only sane person in the car. Perhaps I'll shut up so I don't entice him to drive even faster.

We zip down the road for another fifteen minutes, speeding like crazy through the sharp curves, while S and Cecil breed a variety of useless conversations. I sit quietly, holding on to what appears to be the final moments of my life, as I slide around helplessly on the brown and half-peeled vinyl seat. I get this feeling that things couldn't possibly get worse, and that's when the warm golden sunshine disappears behind a chain of dreadful black storm clouds, and the sky starts dumping rain on us.

"Dang it," S spouts angrily. "The stupid windshield wipers ain't working. I can't see a dang thing."

"Then we better just pull this thing over till the rain stops," I say.

S glances at me in the rearview mirror and grins. He cranks the side window down and pokes half of his face out to see, while his foot pumps the brake pedal until it smacks against the floorboard. "That ain't gonna work," he says. "Hope you two ain't got anybody waiting for you in Griggs Town. If I have to pull the emergency brake on this wet road, we might end up off a cliff somewhere."

"Don't be a stupid idiot; just gear the transmission down. You can't be that stupid!" Cecil shouts.

S primes his speech with a wicked laugh. "Oh, come on now, relax. I'm only getting you going. The foot brake never worked. But that gear down thing is a clever idea, though; don't know why I never thought of it." He yanks the shifter, forces the transmission into a lower gear, and the car at once begins to slow. He clicks the emergency brake to slow us down the rest of the way until we finally come to a stop in a small grass lot on the side of the road. My heart rate returns to something like normal as S turns the key and shuts down the engine. He cranks the window back up and pats his waterlogged face with what appears to be a mustard-stained napkin. "Guess we'll just have to sit here till the rain lets up." Cecil and I nod our heads in obvious agreement with him.

We sit in silence for the next few minutes as the rain pours down. Cecil and S gaze at the rain-battered windshield, each appearing to be deep in thought, while I relax and mentally celebrate that the car is no longer in motion.

"I got it!" S says, as he forces a disgusting wad of phlegm from deep within his chest and spits into the same napkin that he just used to wipe his face. "I saw a man do it once. All we have to do is round us up some string—or even a little rope—and tie it to the wiper arms. We can work the wipers manually, as they call it. All we have to do is turn some strings into a motor, and we'll be in business. Cecil can grab ahold of the rope and yank the wipers to one side, while you in the back grab the other rope and yank them to the other side. Back and forth and back and forth."

"That's the worst idea I've ever heard, so you can count me out on that one," I say.

S appears insulted but tries to coerce Cecil into agreement. Cecil chuckles and says, "Yeah, right; there isn't anybody in their right mind going to think that's a good idea. That is a stupid idea."

"Okay, then. If that's how you see it, I'll just figure it out myself. You two can walk the rest of the way to Griggs Town for all I care."

"Bull crap. I done paid you for gas. Why don't you wait till the rain lets up?" Cecil says in a surprisingly calm tone of voice, but I half expect him to lose his temper at any moment. I sure hope he doesn't.

"You better think again, Cecil," S says. "I've already run out that five in gas." S then spits on his thumb and uses it to mop the yellow stains from the corner of the instrument panel. "We've already traveled a good thirty-five miles, and I'm not sitting around here waiting for the rain to stop. It could rain on till next week."

Cecil's face flushes red with anger, and he looks over and stares S right in the eyes. "Well, S, it was nice knowing you, but I guess we'll be getting out right here. Just so you know, I think that is about the stupidest name there ever was. I reckon that S stands for stupid. Best of luck to ya." He pops the handle and shoves the door open. "Come on, Greenway, let's go. Let 'em get in a wreck and die all by himself."

I happily exit the car into the pouring rain and hand Cecil his bag. Cecil grabs the car door and slams it shut with so much force that a piece of rust from the side of the door breaks free and flies to the rear of the car. Cecil bursts out laughing about the rust, and we take off running. We hurry a few feet into the edge of the woods and crawl up under a short, full-bodied magnolia tree, trying to avoid the rain. It is raining so hard that I doubt it will help. But we force ourselves through some of the lower-hanging branches and press ourselves up against the trunk of the tree. The magnolia leaves aren't big enough to shelter us from the rain, but they do at least manage to shield us from the direct hits of the heavy drops by breaking their fall and turning them into small streams of water before they are dumped on our heads and shoulders and down our backs.

We sit and watch as water beads up and streams from the hood and bumper of S's old rag of a car. "I wonder why he is still sitting in the car. I thought he was in some big hurry," Cecil says. He squeegees the rain from his forehead with the side of his hand. "Probably because he thought he was going to stay dry and send me and you out there like idiots to string up them wipers."

"You know he did," I agree. "But I'm just glad we got out when we did—something isn't right about that guy."

We watch for S to do something, but a good ten minutes pass, and he still doesn't budge. "What do you suppose he's doing?" Cecil chuckles. "I ain't ever seen nothing like that guy before. He's nuts. I reckon he got lost in that mound of sausage cans and trash on the floor of his car." Cecil starts laughing again, and this time he has me laughing along with him. We wait and watch for a few more minutes until we see the first sign of movement coming from the car.

"Look! Look, Greenway. He's getting out—watch him. He has a handful of string. I think he's going for it—watch him."

7

The rain hits S's poor head and slips down his long black hair like a waterfall as he exits the car. "Pour it on me, why don't you? Go ahead and pour it on me. Stupid rain!" he shouts, throwing a temper tantrum, stomping and kicking the puddles of water under his feet. Cecil and I try to muffle our laughter so he doesn't hear us, but then we agree there is no point in being quiet about it. "Crap—crap—craaaaap," he chants as he sloshes through the puddles and ties a string to each of the wiper arms. He drops the free end of each string through a crack in the driver's side and passenger side windows and runs to get back into the car. "Stupid rain," he gripes one last time as he slams the driver's side door. And after a few minutes, he cranks the engine and slowly rolls away.

Cecil and I burst out with laughter. "That's one special person right there," Cecil chuckles sarcastically. "We'll see somebody shoveling his rear end off the pavement somewhere before it's all over with."

We sit and watch as the rain spills from the sky and streams all over us. I don't suppose that there is a dry piece of clothing or flesh left anywhere on my body, but it doesn't even seem to matter to me. All I can think is that if we keep having problems like this slow us down, we are never going to make it to Griggs Town in enough time to claim our jobs at the silver mine. I start to feel hopeless about it all and try to consider our options, but my mind draws a blank. "What do you think we should do now?" I ask.

"I don't know, but I don't suppose that we have much choice other than to sit back and hope that the rain lets up. It's hard to tell, but it looks like the sky is trying to clear over yonder." He pauses to point at a vague strip of blue sky in the distance and says, "Hopefully it lets up. But either way, it's going to be dark before long, and I think we need to find somewhere that's out of the rain to dry ourselves off and camp for the night."

"Yeah, I see what you're saying, but I'm starting to worry that we aren't going to make it to Griggs Town in time. We ought to keep going, but I guess we can't walk all night in the pouring rain. Also, I don't know how we are going to find a dry place to camp out here in the middle of nowhere."

As I wait for Cecil to suggest our next move, I start to feel uncomfortable up against this tree. I can't seem to adjust myself out of this awkward bind that keeps sending my legs to sleep. Cecil stares me down as I rub my legs, trying to wake them.

"Do you see that?" he asks, spotting something while watching me rub my sleepy legs. I'm uncertain what he is talking about, but before I can even ask for clarity, he slings his arm through a layer of dripping magnolia branches and points off somewhere to the right of him. I try to follow his finger, but I can't see what he's pointing at. "That's a chimney," he says. "Maybe it's a chimney on an old, abandoned house or something, and we can get out of the rain."

He crawls out from under the tree. "Let's go take a look at it. Are you coming?" Thunder rumbles in the sky as I crawl out behind him. "Leave our bags there," he says. "We can come back for them in a minute. Let's hurry and check this out." I follow Cecil through the pouring rain along a short path around an overgrown thicket. "Good golly," Cecil says as we approach a brick chimney standing like a lonely totem pole. "That ain't nothing but a chimney; there's no dang house. Where in the world is it? How can there be a chimney but no house? That's the craziest thing I ever saw."

"Maybe the house burnt down," I suggest.

"I don't see anything burnt down—no ashes or any other signs of it—and the chimney ain't even burnt at all."

"Maybe it burnt down a long time ago. That looks like the remains of the foundation, where the house used to be," I say as I point to a row of perfectly laid rectangular gray stones. "If you look closely, you can see all four corners of the house. And look at the size of that tree within the old foundation. That's got to be at least fifty years old. Every bit of fifty years, if not more. Right there where the house would have been sitting."

Cecil shakes his head in disbelief and wrings the water from his shirttail, even though the rain continues to fall. "Well, that just blows my mind. It's like the forest is taking this land back."

I spot a structure through the surrounding trees. "Look, Cecil. There is something over there. Is that what I think it is?" I guide him with my finger, and he confirms my thought.

"I see it. I guess the forest hasn't reclaimed everything just yet. But from here it looks like it's only an old johnny house. It won't do us much good, though. I ain't going in there." As we move closer to investigate, we spot another structure. "Look, there's a little shed or a building out behind it," Cecil says. "Let's go get our bags. It will be dry in there."

Cecil and I fetch our feed bags, pull the door open, and hurry into the rickety building. A few rusty farm implements dangle from the rafters, and concrete blocks are stacked in one corner, but otherwise the building is vacant. "Well, it's got half a roof left on her," Cecil says, inspecting the rusted, half-missing, and peeling tin roof panels. "And that's more than enough roof to get us out of the rain."

"It will just be great to be able to change out of these wet clothes and dry out," I say.

"That's what I'm thinking, but let's build us a fire first—we will dry out quicker around a fire, won't we?"

"How do you figure on doing that? Are you talking about building a fire in here?"

"Well, genius, we can't get one going out there in the rain. This here's a dirt floor, and the other end of the building is missing the roof. I think we ought to be able to build a little fire over there, just a piece out of the rain."

"Don't you think it will smoke us out of here?"

"No way!" Cecil says with confidence. But the expression on his face doesn't seem to share the same level of confidence as his mouth. "I don't see how it will smoke us out, but it isn't going to hurt us to try. If it does, we can just kick it over and let the rain put the fire out."

I nod in agreement, and we start stripping a few of the long planks of siding from the walls of the building. We prop the planks up on the edge of the concrete blocks and stomp on them until we break them in half and arrange them loosely on the dirt floor. And after a few tries, Cecil ignites one of the flimsy cardboard matches that he got from Mr. Jenny's store and starts the fire. "And that's how you do it," Cecil boasts. "She's blazing now."

In less than a minute, and just as I had figured, the small building fills with thick, white smoke. "I don't want to hear one word from you about it—not one word," Cecil gripes. I snicker.

"What's so doggone funny?" he asks.

"Nothing," I say, trying to hide my grin.

"It ain't that doggone funny," he says, but he manages to smile while saying it.

"Maybe if we can see to kicking that door open, some of the smoke will clear out of here," I suggest.

Cecil feels his way to the door and opens it, creating a draft that causes the smoke to swirl around for a few seconds before it is sucked out of the roof. "It will probably stop smoking when the fire gets going good," he says.

We stand in silence for the next few minutes and watch as the fire skips across the wood planks and grows hotter. "See there," Cecil says, "I told you it would stop. It isn't smoking at all now." He pulls the door shut. "Look! The smoke is pulling out of the hole in the roof—just like a chimney now."

We strip off our wet clothes, wring them out, and sling them over the dusty rafters on the dry side of the building. Then we dig through our pig feed bags, pull out a dry change of clothes, and start getting dressed. "I must admit that we look like idiots carrying around these bags that say PIG FEED on them, but at least they're waterproof. Everything in my bag is good and dry," Cecil says. "But I don't even remember packing all this crap. What in the world is all this?"

"The reason you don't remember is because you were mad when you were packing. You were just cramming stuff in there."

"I reckon I was, but I ain't got no use for half of it. Look here, I must have worn these pair of jeans when I was a kid." Cecil unfolds a short tan-colored pair of slacks and holds them up.

"Look how little they are. I didn't even know I had these short little britches."

"Ha, those jeans aren't yours. I promise you they aren't," I say, trying my best to hide my laughter, but unable to hold it back but for a half a second because Cecil is a good six feet tall, and those pants are fit for a fourth grader. The confused look on his face is priceless.

"I reckon they must be. If they ain't, then whose are they? They were in my dresser."

"Just look at them for a minute and think about it. We didn't have pants like that when we were kids, and if we did, they would be loaded from belt loop to ankle with holes and grass stains. As sure as I'm standing here, those are your cousin's britches. There isn't a soul in all of Colby Valley, other than your favorite cousin, Bobby, who owns a pair of tan britches. And that is just about his size."

By this point my laughter is starting to sputter out of control. But Cecil shoots me a serious, squinty-eyed look, as if to say I had better shut up.

He pauses for a moment and appears to think. He looks at the pants again and then stares at me as if I am a suspect. "Well, how in the world did they wind up mixed in with my clothes? Did you do this?"

"I didn't have anything to do with it. You were the one that packed your bag—not me. And you know that Cousin Bobby was always going through your things, and he must have traded a pair of his pants for yours."

"My pants are too big for him, but I guess that won't stop that idiot from wearing them. You just wait till I get ahold of that boy," Cecil growls. I try not to laugh, but once again I can't help it. He shrinks his lips, stares me down as if he is about to charge at me, and says, "What are you laughing about, anyway? It ain't that doggone funny. Don't make me kick your butt, and you know I can do it. I'm wet and tired and don't feel like it, so knock it off."

Cecil tries to resist a smile, so I know that his feelings can't be too hurt over it. "Sorry, Cecil. I don't mean to laugh, but you would be laughing, too, if I had been lugging around the cousin's britches on my back all day, especially your favorite Cousin Bobby's britches."

"Now, dang it, Greenway—shut up already. I'll show you." He grabs the short tan britches by one of the cuffs and slings them and cracks them like a whip at me. He misses me but then continues to chase me around the fire a few times with two more attempts at the whip. By this point we are both giggling like children. And I am in tears from laughing over it. He spikes Cousin Bobby's pants into the fire, and we giggle as the fire dances across the short tan britches, turning them into a distant memory.

"What did you do that for?" I ask. "Little Bobby is going to be sore when he finds out what you did."

"All right, already—the jokes on me. Now knock it off, or you're going in the fire next."

"Okay," I say. "Truce. What do you say we eat some supper and forget about it?" I toss Cecil a can of potted meat along with a sleeve of saltine crackers, and we kneel down by the fire to eat. As I eat, I peek through a gap in the building's splintered chestnut .siding and watch as the rain ends and the cloud-covered sun slides behind the trees.

The sky shifts from dim to dark, and the sound of singing crickets fills the night. But then a troubling noise carries through the darkness. "Listen," I say. "I hear sirens or something—do you hear it?"

"Yeah, it sounds like a boatload of cop cars, fire trucks, or ambulances, doesn't it?"

"That's exactly what it is. And that is about the last thing I would expect to hear out here in the middle of nowhere." I pause for a moment and listen as the noise grows closer and closer. Various possible reasons for a convoy of emergency vehicles coming this way cross my mind. "Hey, Cecil. Are you by any chance thinking what I'm thinking?"

"I don't know. What are you thinking?"

"Do you think them sirens have anything to do with S and those homemade windshield wipers? It seems to me like it would be hard to hold a steering wheel while playing puppeteer with the windshield wipers."

"Oh crap! I'll bet it does have something to do with him. I'll bet that dummy done got himself killed. I'll bet he did. That's terrible. There hasn't been more than two cars on this road all day, so why else would there be sirens?"

We listen for the next several seconds, quietly chewing our crackers so that we don't miss any new noises. And after about a minute, what sounds like four or five emergency vehicles blast their sirens as they speed past us on the nearby road. Cecil grabs the water jug, washes down a mouthful of crackers, and says, "Yep. It sounds like they are heading right for him—right in his direction. They'll be scraping him off the pavement just like I reckoned they would. I got half a mind to go hunt him down and get our five dollars back before they haul him away."

That's an awful thing to say, I think, but I don't see the point of saying anything about it. I stare across the fire at Cecil as he crams another load of crackers into his cheeks. A different noise interrupts my stare. "Stop messing with the cracker bag for a second," I say. "Please stop. I hear something right outside the building; it sounds like somebody stomping on the ground or something. Did you hear that?"

"I don't hear anything but the fire popping."

"No. That isn't what I heard; it's something else."

Cecil laughs, shakes his head, and mumbles through a mouthful of crackers, "Maybe that dummy S came back from the dead to haunt us. If he did, I hope he's got our five dollars on him."

"Stop playing, Cecil. I'm being serious."

He rolls his eyes and chomps his crackers as something hits the side of the building. *Thump—thump.* "What in the world was that, Greenway? You weren't kidding; there is something out there." He pulls a half-burnt plank of wood from the fire and holds it up like a torch. "Whatever it is, it's about to be sorry it ever met me."

Cecil stands up, inches to the door, and grips the smoking plank of half-burning wood above his shoulder like a baseball bat. I grab a small concrete block from the corner of the building and join him. It is silent for a moment, but then the voice of a man ricochets through the shack's walls. "You got thirty seconds to put that fire out and get off my property before I kill ya!"

I look at Cecil and he looks at me. Cecil whispers, "Don't you move. If he comes through that door, you just nail him with that block while I get him with this board."

"No," I whisper. "That's a terrible idea. Why don't we just leave? If it's his property, we don't have the right to be here."

"Because any man who threatens to kill you without ever laying eyes on you ain't right in the head. We're not causing any trouble, and you can't just walk up to somebody and start talking trash like that. That ain't normal. You just stay right here and do as I tell you."

The man outside starts counting. "One Mississippi . . . two Mississippi . . . three Mississippi . . . four—"

Cecil grunts, forces air through his nostrils like a bull, and starts shouting, "I've had about all this threatening from you that I'm going to take!" He kicks the door of the building open and yells, "You just step right in here and find out!" All I can do is raise the concrete block over my head and prepare for the worst.

"Hey, just hold on a second—take it easy," the man says. "I'm only playing around. It's me, S—you know, the fella that you hitched a ride from earlier."

S peeks through the door and reveals his face in the flickering firelight. "Oh, doggone it," Cecil says. "You're crazy. That didn't even sound like you. You 'bout got your head knocked clear off your shoulders messing around like that. And what do you want? I thought you were in a hurry to be somewhere? But then again, we thought you were dead because of all those sirens."

"Well, I was in a hurry, and I still am. But that whole windshield wiper thing didn't work out too well. I came close to running over an embankment down the way. I had to pull her off the road, and now she's stuck in the mud. Do you have room in there for one more?"

"I doubt it," Cecil says, crossing his arms and staring S dead in the eye. "You put us out in the pouring rain earlier after ripping us off for five bucks, and so it seems to me that you just need to move on."

"Oh, come on, Cecil. Nobody's perfect. I'm only human and don't always do as I should. I mean, come on—how about a little forgiveness? I'll tell you what, I'll make it up to you and take you the rest of the way to Griggs Town—I promise."

I don't trust the man one bit and don't want him in here, but I don't feel the need to speak up, because there is no way Cecil is going to let him come in after the way he done us. I brace myself for more confrontation as Cecil begins to speak up again. "Well," he says, "you sure don't deserve it, but if I don't let you in, that'll make me about as awful as you—so get in here."

Cecil steps away from the door and lets S walk in. I drop my head down, unwilling to even make eye contact with the man. And I am speechless over Cecil's response. Never in a million years would I have figured that my hot-headed brother would have let S through that door. I'm all about forgiveness, but trust is a different thing altogether. S walks past me and flops down in the dirt by the fire.

"Where's your car?" Cecil asks.

"Well, I parked her about a quarter mile down the road."

"So why did you come back here?"

"I thought I was going to stay with the car, but I don't have any food and ain't had anything to eat in a while. And I was hoping that if I could find y'all, you might have some to share."

"You don't deserve it, but I suppose you can have a little—not that we can afford to spare much."

"Shoot. I knew all along you had a heart," S says. "You got spirit, too—and maybe even a bit of a temper, but you got heart. So, what kind of food do you got?"

To my surprise, Cecil reaches over and offers him a handful of food. "Here, I reckon you can have this can of meat and a few crackers. But if you want something to drink, you'll have to fetch yourself some rainwater. I ain't drinking after you, so you can't have our jug."

"That sounds fair to me. I don't know how to thank you." He scrapes his fingers through his black hair, flips the rain from it, and says, "I'm sure glad y'all got a fire. If it wasn't for all that smoke, I might have never found you." He rips the lid from the can of potted meat and sniffs. "Man, oh man! That smells good," he says. "I never thought I'd be so excited to see a can of spotted dog." He scoops up the flesh-colored paste with his fingers, and in two bites it's gone. "What's wrong with your brother?" he says. "He ain't spoke a word since I been here. I get the feeling he isn't too happy with me being here."

"I don't know. Why don't you ask him?"

"You all right over there, Green Beret . . . Greenway, or whatever your name is?"

"I suppose," I say with my eyes still fixed on the dirt floor, having no desire whatsoever to even look at him.

"Well, you don't say much."

"What can I say? I guess I don't feel the need to say anything."

He stuffs his mouth full of crackers. "Don't know how you expect to make friends in life acting like that," he says.

"Well, if we are being honest, I don't care about making any friends. The only thing I care about is making it to Griggs Town."

"What are you two so bent on getting to Griggs for? Why you going?"

"For work," I say.

"Shoot, you mean to tell me you're traveling all the way to Griggs just for work? Work is overrated. I haven't had a job in years," he says, smiling and aiming his malicious eyes at my can of potted meat.

Cecil says, "Well, S, now that you brought it up, why is it that you're going to Griggs? Since you clearly aren't going for work."

"No. I ain't got no work there. I'm just going for a visit."

"Just a visit? What, do you have family there?"

"Who, me? No, I don't have anyone there. I'm just going there for the scenery. I'm taking a little vacation, you might say."

"What scenery?" Cecil asks.

"There is some pretty country out there; just figured I'd take a look around—some pretty women too."

"What?! You've been there before?"

"Nope. I've never been there, but I sure have read about her. They say she's a real good-looking place. Look here—I got an article about her if the rain didn't ruin it." He pulls out his wallet, removes a small piece of paper, and unfolds it. "Look like she's still dry—want me to read her to ya?"

"Go for it," Cecil says. "We ain't got anything better to do."

"I'm a little slow at reading, but here it goes:

At the foothills of the Appalachian Mountains in Eastern Kentucky sits a place that is known as "the birthplace of Southern hospitality," a place called Griggs Town. The entrance to Griggs Town is characterized by steep mountains and old-growth forest, with many of the town's trees towering over 100 feet tall, while the rest of the town is distinguished by beautiful flower gardens, stone-railed bridges, and the spring-fed streams that pour into the town's 170-acre water reservoir.

A flagstone walkway surrounds the reservoir, while wooden platforms branch out from the walkway and lead you to clumps of freshly painted storefronts and brick-paved alleyways. The reservoir is known as the heart of town, and almost everything that Griggs Town has to offer, including restaurants, shops, and churches, can be found here.

And it's not only the scenery and the atmosphere that make Griggs Town the hidden treasure that it is; it is the people, as well. When we visited Griggs Town this week, everyone we talked to spoke to us like they had known us our whole lives. We talked to several shop owners, town employees, and the mayor's daughter, and they told us—

He stops reading midsentence and says, "Well, what do you think? She sure sounds pretty, doesn't she?"

"Yeah, but keep on reading," I say.

"Sorry, but that was the end of it."

"That can't be," Cecil says. "Sounds to me like you quit right in the middle. Let me see that thing." S hesitates for a second but agrees and hands Cecil the paper.

He strips the paper from S's hand and scrutinizes it. "You can't be serious," Cecil blurts. "It says right here, 'continued on page four.' I take it you don't have page four, do you?"

"Nope, that's all I got. Not sure what I did with page four."

"Well, thanks," I say as sarcastically as possible. "You get us real interested in something that you can't even complete."

"Sorry, there, Green Beret. I can make up an ending for you if you want." He cackles, slaps himself on the side of the leg, and says, "Well, do you want me to? I think I could make up something real nice."

"Don't bother with it," I say. "I'll get to see Griggs Town soon enough."

Unfortunately, I am forced to endure the rest of the evening listening to S's far-fetched stories. He even tries to tell us that he was once a helicopter pilot, a bull rider, and even a professional race-car driver. But I don't have any reason to believe that he is telling us the truth, because he just doesn't come across as an honest person to me. But his mouth goes on and on and doesn't stop until Cecil calls him a liar and gets him to be quiet long enough so that we can try to go to sleep. I am relieved that his mouth is shut, but I'm still not sure how I'm going to be able to fall asleep with this crazy man in here with us.

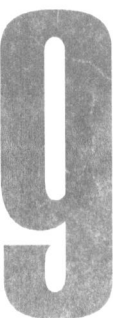

The following morning, a beam of sunlight pricks through a crack in the wall of the building, and the warmth of the beam crawls across my face and wakes me. I roll over, and the first thing I notice is that S is gone. I'm thinking that he must have stepped out to use the restroom, but if I'm lucky, Cecil may have gotten him so sore from calling him a liar last night that he left us for good. I don't know, but I hope he doesn't come back; I sure don't want to risk getting back into that miserable car of his again.

While fantasizing that S will never return, I look over and laugh as I see Cecil snoring with his foot lying halfway in the smoldering remains of last night's fire. I consider giving him a quick nudge or a shout to wake him, but then again, this may be my opportunity to have a little fun.

Without much thought, I sneak over to the fire and rake a few hot coals over next to Cecil's shoe. I arrange a few small pieces of wood and a pinch of tinder on the coals, and with a quick burst of air from my lungs, a small flame rises next to his foot. I hurry back to where I was and lie back down. I pretend that I am sleeping and peek through one squinty eye, while watching the fire flicker next to Cecil's foot.

The flame grows higher and hotter, and the sole of Cecil's shoe releases a plume of black smoke. I watch with anticipation, hoping that the heat wakes him up before his entire shoe erupts in flames. But as he continues to snore, I get the feeling that I've done a terrible thing, and that I may have to wake him to keep him from getting burnt. But then his eyes pop open, and he jumps to his feet. "WHAT'S GOING ON?! I'M ON FIRE! I'M ON FIRE!" he shouts. He stomps his foot on the floor to kill the flames and then kicks his leg until the melted shoe flies from his foot.

A cloud of steam surrounds Cecil's sock, and it takes every muscle in my face, neck, and even my shoulders to withhold my laughter. "What's going on?" I ask, pretending that he just woke me up, stretching my arms, yawning, and acting confused.

"My stupid foot's on fire is what's going on—and thanks for helping."

"How is your foot on fire? Are you okay?"

"I woke up and my shoe was on fire. Guess I got over too far in the fire in my sleep."

He slides his sock off and inspects his foot. "I guess I'm all right. It just got hot for a second. But man—what a way to wake up. I reckon that's what they mean when they say 'rude awakening.'" He chuckles while fetching his shoe. "I'm just glad I didn't burn my foot off." He kicks the building door open and looks outside. "Where is S?"

I pull myself from the floor and join Cecil as he stands at the door. "Your guess is as good as mine."

He yells out the door, "Hey, S, you out here?"

No reply. The only sounds are a light breeze slipping through the trees and a few distant songbirds.

"I'll bet you he done took off without us, that lying . . . good-for-nothing . . . bum!" Cecil walks over, pees on the hot coals from last night's fire, and continues, "Oh well, at least it's not raining. We better get our bags packed back up and get going 'fore it gets hot out there." He reaches over to pick up his feed sack off the floor and pauses mid reach. "Where is our water jug?" he asks.

I look all around, and it is nowhere to be found. "You have got to be kidding me," I say. "S must have taken off with it."

Cecil gasps, spins around, and scours the floor for other missing items. "This can't be happening," he says. "All of our food's gone too. He took it all! And wait a minute, he even stole our grandpa's pocket watch—our only watch."

"Please tell me you're kidding. It can't be gone!"

"It is," he howls, "it's all gone. But let's hurry and get the rest of our stuff together. If he hasn't been gone for long, we might be able to catch him."

In a matter of seconds, we have our remaining belongings packed into our bags and we are sprinting through the woods. "I'm going to punch him right between the eyes just as soon as I see him!" Cecil shouts.

"Not if I get to him first."

And after being smacked by a hundred tree branches and stabbed by a dozen briar bushes, we make it to the edge of the road. Cecil darts into the middle of the road, stops for a second, and looks around. "Where are you? Where are you?" he screams. "If we hurry, we might be able to find his car," he says as he takes off running down the middle of the road.

I follow, and as I run, I scan the edge of the road looking for signs of S. After about ten minutes of solid running, Cecil notices something lying in the middle of the road and stops to see what it is. "Look at this." He snatches it from the pavement and slings it at me. "This is what's left of one of our apples that thief stole."

"This must be where S ditched his car last night," I say. "You can almost see the tire tracks in the grass, and that right there is the rope from his windshield wipers."

Cecil walks to the rope, picks it up, and inspects it. "It sure is," he says, as he wads it up and shoves it in his sack. "But don't you worry about it. He'll get his day—he'll pay for this."

We spend the rest of the day walking along the highway and talking about S. I try to forget about him and focus on Griggs Town, but my hunger pains and thirsty lips won't let me. The occasional traveler that drives by and ignores our hitchhiking thumbs takes my mind off him for about a minute, but as soon as they get out of sight, my angry stomach screams his name into my ears again. And after one of the longest and most miserable days of walking that I have ever known, I finally hear the sound that I have been longing for: the sweet sound of water gurgling and skipping across a stony creek bed. Without a moment of discussion, Cecil and I leave the road to investigate the refreshing noise.

A jungle of mountain laurels obscures our view of the stream, so we slip through the thick laurel branches, using our ears to guide us. "Thank God," Cecil shouts as we emerge from the jungle and see a stream. "I was afraid my ears were lying to me."

I drop my bag to the ground and then almost trip over it as I hurry toward the stream to drink. I scoop up the water with my hands and slurp as Cecil sloshes to the middle of the stream and drops down on his belly in the rapids. He opens his mouth to drink and laughs as the water rushes in.

This water is as clean and refreshing as melted snow and, although flavorless, the best water that I've ever tasted. I don't understand how something so tasteless can, at the same time, taste so delicious. I don't know, but this water must be a gift from God.

No sooner has my stomach been satisfied with its desire for water than it begins to grumble for food. "Hey, Cecil, do you think there are any fish in these waters?"

Cecil emerges from the stream in dripping clothes and says, "This isn't that much of a stream, but it doesn't take much for fish. I reckon there could be. There could be trout or something in one of these holes. Trout live in places like this."

"Well, why don't we see if we can catch a couple and cook them up for supper?"

Cecil stares me down as if I have said something stupid. "Okay, genius. What are we going to catch them with—our looks?"

"I don't know. But there has to be a way to do it, don't you think?"

"Yeah, I have the perfect idea," Cecil says with a hint of sarcasm, slowly clapping his hands.

"You do?"

"Yeah, let me see your fishing pole, and I'll hook us some right up."

"What fishing pole?"

Cecil looks at me like I'm an idiot and says, "That's my point, dummy. As long as we don't have no fishing pole, we won't be catching anything. We're gonna have to find something else to eat, and that's all there is to it."

"But people in the old days used to use spears," I say. "I think that's how the Indians use to do it. Can't we just sharpen up a stick and spear one?"

"Well, first off, you'll have to be able to see them in order to do that, but we can give it a try."

Cecil breaks a branch from a slender maple tree and tries to sharpen one end of it with his pocketknife. "The wood is too green, and I can't get a sharp point on it," he whines before slinging his pocketknife at me. "There, you can try it. I'm not trying to starve to death, so I'm just going to sneak over here in the woods and see what I can find us before it gets dark. I will have better luck taking a rock to a squirrel or something."

Cecil takes off tiptoeing through the woods, searching for who knows what, as I search for a better spearing stick. I find a long, thin branch that looks and feels like it is dry. With little effort, I manage to carve a sharp point on one end. I step quietly along the edge of the stream with my spear positioned, ready to strike. My empty stomach fills with jitters as I spot a decent-sized fish hovering in a deep hole below a short set of rapids. Before he sees me, I sneak up on him, launch my spear . . . and miss. I rescue the bloodless spear from the water, kneel down, and wait for him to return.

A few minutes later, he returns with two other fish by his side. I begin thinking that my luck is about to change. I draw back my spear, trying to restrain this nervous shake that is developing in my arm. But before I am able take aim, I notice that the tip of my spear is broken off. I hurry to resharpen it. However, before I can even get two layers of wood peeled off, Cecil starts shouting, "Hey, where are you?" I ignore him and continue sharpening the spear. But then he shouts, "Get over here and help me! I got us some supper."

The word *supper* is all I needed to hear, so I abandon my spear and take off running through the woods to find Cecil, and after yelling back and forth for a few times, I find him. But his hands are empty. "Well, where is the food? What did you get?" I ask.

"It's right here—look up in that tree."

"What is it? I don't see anything."

"I ain't sure what it is, but I chased it up that tree."

"You don't know what it is, and you don't even have it? What in the world is wrong with you? I was close to spearing a big fish—there were three of them."

"Forget the stupid fish. This is much bigger. Big enough for supper and even breakfast in the morning. If you stand where I'm at, you can see it. I think it might be a raccoon. Don't you see it? It's black and gray." Cecil guides my eyes with his finger, and I see something but can't tell what it is.

"How do you figure on getting it out of that tree?" I ask.

"I need you to boost me up to that first branch, and then I'll go up there and get it—but hurry, before it gets dark on us."

I give him a boost and watch as he maneuvers up the tree and almost disappears behind the leafy branches. A few seconds later, a sharp growl resonates throughout the woods, and a creature tumbles through the branches and falls to the ground, landing on its feet. The creature and I make eye contact for a second, and then it twirls and takes off running.

"You have got to be kidding me," I shout. "I sure hope you're proud of yourself."

Cecil hurries down the tree and drops to the ground. "What are you talking 'bout? Proud of myself for what? Where'd it go?"

"I don't know, but if I had to guess, I'd say that the little critter ran all the way home."

"You big dummy. You should have knocked him out."

"Well, for one, when he hit the ground, it was only a second before he took off running; and for two, even if I could've knocked him out, there is no way in the world I would have done it."

"Why not? Are you crazy or something? Aren't you hungry? How in the world do you expect us to eat now?"

"Yeah, if you would have just left me alone, I would have had a fish or two and had them frying by now. But no, I had to come over here and help the mighty hunter slaughter somebody's little kitty cat."

"Don't be dumb. That wasn't nobody's kitty cat, and you know it. That was a raccoon. I know what I saw."

"Ha! It's a funny thing how it had a pink collar with a row of bells on it. I never seen a raccoon with bells on it before."

I think Cecil knows that I am telling the truth, but to avoid shame he is not willing to let it go. "I'm telling you, that wasn't no kitty cat. You're crazy," he says.

"Good grief. If the way it growled wasn't enough to prove it to you, then I think the way its little gold bells jingled when it fell through the tree branches would have told you. Not to mention, its tail was solid white. What kind of racoon has a solid white tail?"

"All right. Let's just drop it.— There ain't no point in arguing about it. We might as well get back to the stream and try to catch some fish."

We stomp back toward the stream, and after a brief period of disorientation, we find the part of the stream that we were at before, which is a good thing because this is where we left our feed sacks. But by now, the sun has almost faded, and the possibility of spearing a fish for supper is out of the question. I am so furious with him.

It has been more than a day without any food, and the hunger pains are starting to set in. I am feeling a type of weakness within me that I have never felt before. I begin to think maybe it's possible that I will starve to death. I'm trying my best to keep my cool about the situation, but this severe desperation for food has me on the borderline of panicking. But I suppose that my only option is to load my belly full of water and call it a night. I hope and pray that I will be able to catch a fish or two in the light of morning.

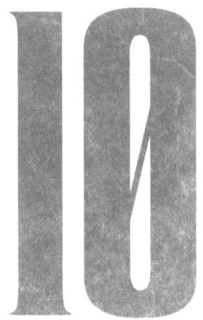

The next morning is filled with nothing but a bunch of unsuccessful spearfishing, as well as a bunch of arguing about the right way to hold and throw a spear. Even though it appears to me that we are about to starve to death, Cecil seems pleased that the whole spearfishing thing isn't working out for us. I guess it makes him feel better about the useless cat chase that we went on the night before.

I try to fight it, but this unmistakable feeling of terror over my hunger pains starts pinching at my soul. Then these crazy thoughts about dying begin to fill my head. I imagine expressions of grief in Mom's and Auntie Rose's faces as they learn of our deaths. And this type of thinking triggers some sort of fight-or-flight instinct, because before I realize what I am doing, I start kicking over rocks, and eating worms and anything else that looks safe to eat. Cecil stares me down as if I've lost my mind, but after a few seconds of observing me, he starts kicking over rocks and eating worms himself.

I manage to find a big beetle, about half as long as my pinky finger, and without even giving it a second thought, I have it wedged between my teeth. Its legs massage my taste buds, as I drop my jaw and send a pile of guts to the back of my tongue. I scoop up a handful of stream water to wash it down and begin searching for another. This scavenger hunt continues for the next few minutes. After Cecil and I agree that we have consumed enough bug meat to no longer die of starvation, we grab our feed sacks and head for the road to continue our journey to Griggs Town.

After a brief period of walking with the hot sun bearing down on us, I look over and notice that Cecil's face is beginning to look a little bit pale. His fast steps turn into more of a slow shuffle, and he comes to a complete stop in the middle of the road. With his feet straddling the two center yellow lines painted on the pavement, he drops his feed sack to the ground, looks over at me, and scoops his belly with the palm of his hand and pukes. I watch as bits and pieces of half-chewed worms twitch and roll in the pool of vomit, and before I even have time to try and talk myself out of it, I find myself emptying my own stomach. "What the heck are we going to do now?" Cecil cries. He pauses to wipe the worm guts from his chin with his arm, and continues, "I guess it's like we never ate at all, and I guess that means we are going to die from starvation again, doesn't it?"

"I don't know, Cecil, but to tell you the truth, I was doing fine until you started throwing up. It wasn't bothering me at all. As crazy as it sounds, we probably should have let our bugs settle a bit before we went out in the heat like that. I think it was the heat that made you sick."

"Yeah, that does sound crazy, but it's a little too late for that now. I'm not feeling too well, and my head is spinning. What am I going to do?"

"Well, the first thing you need to do is find some shade and sit down for a few minutes and get yourself together."

"I'd say you're right about that."

Cecil scoops his feed sack from the pavement, takes off walking, and I follow him to the edge of the road. We sprawl out on our backs under a large shade tree, with our heads resting on our feed sacks. And after a few minutes, Cecil cocks his head sideways and peers at me out of the corner of his eye. "What?" I ask.

"I smell something, Greenway." He pokes his nose toward the sky, sniffs rapidly, and announces, "I smell fried chicken—"

"Yeah, right," I say, assuming that Cecil's sickness is just making him delusional. "I'll bet you smell all those bug guts over there roasting on the pavement."

He sniffs again and pauses, then sniffs again and pauses, and says, "Nah, I know what I smell. It's fried chicken, and I know it. I may not be good at a lot of things, but my nose has never let me down. Do you remember when we were kids, how I used to smell Mom's cooking from halfway across the holler?"

"Yeah."

"Well, this is one of those times."

"Okay, then where is it coming from? I sure don't smell anything—"

"Hold on, I hear something too—just listen a minute."

At first, all I can hear are the sounds of our stomachs growling, but as I listen more closely, I get excited as I hear the faint sounds of car doors slamming and an engine starting. And a few seconds later, I hear the broken pitches of a woman's voice and the depth of a man's voice.

"I wonder what all that's about," Cecil says.

"I don't know, but we're about as close to the middle of nowhere as we can get. There is no telling what it is—though, it could be S."

Without another drop of discussion, we take off down the road and head toward the mixture of noises and the alleged scents of fried chicken. And once we learn where it's all coming from, we can't believe our eyes.

"Please tell me my eyes aren't playing tricks on me," Cecil says. "It's a store and a restaurant. I told you I smelt fried chicken. I told you. I knew it was fried chicken!"

I burst out in laughter.

"What's so funny?" Cecil asks.

"Don't you realize that we came close to starving to death? And there we were, cramming bugs in our mouths and everything, and all the while, we were sitting right next door to a restaurant."

Cecil smacks me on the back of the head and says, "You idiot." He laughs and struggles for a moment to compose himself. "I guess you're right, and it's kind of funny when you put it that way. But it was your dumb idea to start eating bugs in the first place. That was so dumb. But let's stash our sacks in a ditch and go in here and get us something real to eat."

"All right, but first let's see how much money we got."

Cecil reaches into his pocket and pulls out a wad of crinkled bills and some change. "We got six-seventy," he says. "Do you want me to count it again, or can we eat already?"

"Okay. I just wanted to make sure that S didn't steal that too."

We avoid the expensive and delicious scents that bleed through the gaps in the restaurant's rusty tin roof and hurry into the store. Without much debate, we settle for the cheapest thing on the shelf: potted meat and crackers. And we manage to leave with about half a bag of it, two jugs of water, and a little bit of change leftover.

As soon as we set foot outside the store, we come face-to-face with a gorgeous, well-dressed woman. She looks to be in her middle to late twenties, with light auburn hair hanging all the way down to the center of her back and sparkling green eyes. She smiles and says, "Hi there, fellas—new in town?"

Cecil's eyes light up, and he strives to speak, but his drooling tongue won't allow him to say a word.

"No, we're just passing through," I say, completely unintimidated by her beauty; all I can think about at this moment is our bag of potted meat and crackers.

"Where are you heading?" she asks.

"Oh, we're heading to a place called Griggs Town," I say.

"Well, that's a good choice—Griggs Town could use a few handsome fellas such as yourselves."

Cecil manages to unravel his twisted tongue. "Well, thank ya, ma'am. You ain't too bad yourself."

The woman covers her mouth with a cupped hand and giggles. "Thank you, handsome," she purrs. "My name is Meredith."

"That's a fine name. My name's Cecil, and my brother's name here is Greenway."

She runs her open fingers through her hair and pinches it into a ponytail, revealing the sides of her neck. "Do you guys want to hang out?" she asks.

I jump right in, ready to give my thoughts on such a ridiculous question. "Not to be rude, ma'am," I say, "but we don't have the time to hang out. We have to get to Griggs Town because we have a job waiting on us—"

Cecil extends his arm in front of me and motions for me to stop talking. "Yes, of course we would like to hang out," Cecil says, staring at me as if to say, *Ya better keep your mouth shut.* "As a matter of fact," he continues, "we have plenty of time."

I don't know what this woman is up to, but if she had even the slightest idea about the amount of bugs and worm guts that recently crossed our lips, she'd be running in the other direction. The woman releases her ponytail and grabs Cecil's wrist. "You guys come with me so we can hang out somewhere more private."

She leads us down a path beside the store and stops short near a filthy green dumpster. "Okay," she says. "Here is good."

The whites of Cecil's eyes light up. And I tap the side of the paper bag full of meat, trying to remind him of his hunger, but his attention won't focus elsewhere. "What now?" Cecil asks.

"That depends," she says, slowly extending her arm and placing her hand on Cecil's shoulder.

"It depends on what?" Cecil asks.

"Well, it depends on how much money you got."

Cecil's eyes cross as they fill with confusion. "I don't know what that has to do with anything, but if you must know, I think we have about eighty cents left."

"And don't you think about letting her borrow it, either," I say. "We are going to need that eighty cents for a stamp and an envelope, so we can tell Mom and Auntie Rose about that money we hid for them in the barn—remember?"

Meredith removes her hand from Cecil's shoulder. "I think you got it all wrong," she says. "I'm not trying to borrow your money."

"Well then, why are you asking about our money?" Cecil asks.

"Because I'm a prostitute."

"What in the world is that supposed to mean?" Cecil responds, his expression becoming even more puzzled. "I never heard of a prostitute. Is that some sort of a medical condition or something? Do you need money for doctors?"

Meridith's mouth drops open as if she is insulted, and her soft and sweet voice dissolves into a more aggressive tone. "No, I don't have a medical condition. How stupid can you be? That's not what a prostitute is. A prostitute means that I have sex for money."

"Well, uh—um . . . you heard my brother," Cecil says. "We need those eighty cents to send a letter, so I can't be spending it on sex."

Meredith grips her hair into a ponytail again and relaxes against the dumpster. "Honey," she says, "eighty cents wouldn't even cover the cost of me blowing you a kiss."

Cecil steps back, looking disturbed. "I'll be doggone," he says. "I wouldn't pay you a dirty dime for a kiss—not even if you begged me. You ought to have more respect for yourself than to try to sell yourself for money. That ain't something a real woman would ever think about doing. It's just wrong and you ought to be ashamed of it." Cecil turns his disappointed scowl to me and says, "Come on, Greenway. Let's just get out of here before she tries to talk us out of our potted meat and crackers."

We flee from the girl and hurry back around to the front of the store, but before we can even turn the corner, we almost bump into a short, heavyset man with slacks as smooth as paper. He looks as startled as we are, but I notice a sheriff's deputy badge gleaming on his shirt. "You boys hold it right there," he demands. He places his hand on his gun holster and says, "Now, drop the paper bag and jugs and put your hands on the wall right here." I look on in confusion as he taps on the store's painted gray siding. "Right here," he repeats.

We drop our stuff on the ground and place our hands up against the wall. And we watch as he grabs our bag of food and searches through it. "The salesclerk in here says he seen you two boys out front soliciting a prostitute."

"I'm not sure what you're talking about, but I can assure you that we did no such thing," Cecil gripes. "All I know is that she tried to talk us into giving her our money for sex, but we never gave her a dime. And I can promise you that. We just told that old hussy that we were saving our eighty cents for a stamp and an envelope and left her at the dumpster where she belongs. Ask my brother; he'll tell ya."

"It's true," I say. "We had no part in it. We didn't even know what she was trying to do until we followed her out back—and as soon as we found out, we got out of there. That's why we are standing here and not back there with her. I think you ought to go after her instead of us."

"I'll worry about her later," the officer replies. "You are lucky I didn't catch you back there with her or you'd probably be going out of here in handcuffs. Now, let me check and make sure that you got nothing on you that you aren't supposed to, and I will send you on your way. Is it okay if I search you?"

"It's okay with me," I respond.

"All right by me," Cecil says.

He slips on a pair of blue latex gloves and prepares to search me first. "I'm going to reach into your pockets, young man. Now, is there anything in here that's going to poke or stab me—any needles, weapons, or anything like that?"

"No, sir," I say, "no weapons or needles. I have never sewed a thing in my life. If we ever needed something sewed, Mom always did that."

The deputy grins, shakes his head, and pokes his fingers into each of my pants pockets and pats me down my legs and feels around my ankles. "Okay, you're clean—just keep your hands there on the wall for a minute while I check your brother."

He steps over to search Cecil. "Now, I'm going to reach my hands in your pockets—you got any weapons, needles, or anything in there that will poke me?"

"No, sir," Cecil mutters. "There ain't no needles in my pocket. What kind of man carries around sewing stuff in his pocket? I ain't got no sewing stuff, but I got a folding pocketknife in there—and about eighty cents in change."

The deputy grins and chuckles under his breath. "I wasn't asking about sewing needles. I was talking about drug paraphernalia."

"Well, we don't have any of that, either. We ain't on no drugs."

The deputy grins again and starts poking around in Cecil's pockets and slides out Cecil's pocketknife along with the change. He unfolds the pocketknife, inspects the blade, and then slips the pocketknife and the change back into Cecil's pocket. And he pats down Cecil's legs and ankles just like he did me. "It looks like you guys are clean," he says. "Both of you can go ahead and put your hands down."

The deputy turns around and starts to walk away, but after a few steps, he stops, turns back around, and says, "Where are you boys from? It looks like you've been sleeping in a ditch or something."

"We come from Colby Valley," I say. "But we've been on foot for the last few days, trying to make it to Griggs Town."

"Griggs Town—hmm. I hear that a lot of people are going there, Why are you all headed there?"

"We're headed there for work," I say. "We have a job promised to us at the Swift silver mine—that is, if we can ever make it."

The deputy smiles. "Well, you're not that far off. In fact, Griggs Town is just a few miles across the county line—not far from the sheriff's office. I'm headed back that way if you two want to hop in the cruiser. I'll be happy to take you up the road as far as I can." Cecil and I exchange happy smiles, and without question, we agree and get in the car with the deputy.

After maybe half an hour of us chomping potted meat and crackers and chugging water from a gallon jug in the back seat of the police car, the deputy slows down and stops in the middle of nowhere. "All right," he says. "You boys get out here. This is the county line and as far as I can take you. All you have to do is keep in this direction, around that curve, and you'll be in Griggs. It might take you an hour."

He gives us a fair lecture about keeping out of trouble. Once we finish expressing our appreciation for the ride, we exit the car. The deputy waves as he drives off.

After about an hour, we approach a large wooden sign atop two short posts. It is the most beautiful sign that I have ever seen. In hand-carved letters, the sign reads: Welcome to Griggs Town—The Birthplace of Southern Hospitality. Below all those welcoming letters is a beautiful collage of hand-carved buildings, a church with a cross steeple, large trees, a waterfall, and a long, winding stream that spans the length of the sign.

A sense of relief washes over me as I read the words, Welcome to Griggs Town.

"Well, brother. It looks like we made it," I say.

"Yeah, we did."

Cecil reaches over and puts his arm around me, and we admire the sign together. After a few seconds, he reaches his other arm around and punches me in the stomach. "Now, come on, you big dummy. We can't just stand here and stare at the sign all day. Let's go and see what we came here for."

A short distance down the Griggs Town road, the scenery starts to change, and I get the feeling that I am entering a different world. A cold chill slips across my body as densely vegetated mountains hug the shoulders of the road like canyon walls, hiding the warmth of the afternoon sun. As we continue, the vegetation fades, revealing fractured and jagged stone ledges, where water seeps and drips from dark green crevices in the rock.

We stride down a short incline in the road and around a narrow curve until we find ourselves facing a large mountain with a tunnel carved out of it. As I get closer, I can see that a granite plaque is mounted above the center of the tunnel's entrance. The plaque reads: Griggs Mountain Tunnel–1902. Cecil drops his sack and stops in the middle of the road. "Good grief, Greenway. That's one monster tunnel." He's looking kind of pale, and he draws in a deep breath before continuing. "You didn't tell me that we had to go through a stupid tunnel to get into Griggs Town."

"Well, that's because I didn't know there was a tunnel. But boy, it sure is dark in there. You can't even see the other end of it. It must be one long tunnel."

"Shut up, already. You can go first," Cecil says.

Sensing that Cecil is a little nervous and because he is always acting like the tough guy, I decide that now is as good a time as any to pick on him. "What, are you scared of the dark?"

"Don't you mess with me," Cecil barks, before drawing in another deep breath. "I don't like tight spaces—I'm clutterphobic."

"You're clutterphobic? What's that?"

"I'm claustrophobic, you idiot. You know what I'm trying to say."

12

I scan through a lifetime of childhood memories but cannot recall one instance where I remember Cecil being claustrophobic. But I settle on this opportunity to be the braver of the two of us, and I take off walking. I get a little ways into the tunnel and realize I don't hear Cecil's feet shuffling behind me, so I turn around to see where he is and find him still standing at the entrance. "Are you coming or what?"

"I can't do it, Greenway. I just can't."

"Oh, come on. Please. I promise it won't hurt you. It won't take us but a few minutes to make it to the other side. We have to do it. We have a job waiting on us."

I watch for him to move and listen for him to respond, but he doesn't budge. I don't know what to do. He acts like such a tough guy most of the time that I want to keep poking fun at him for being afraid, but I suppose I need to be the better person and try to talk him through this. I must admit, though, it is somewhat harsh seeing my brother, who has spent most of his life displaying this rough and careless image, being forced to show weakness like this.

"Okay, Cecil. I have an idea: you grab ahold of my shirttail and close your eyes, and I will lead you through here. We'll be in and out of here in no time. You won't even have time to think about it."

"Oh sure, genius! Closing my eyes is going to make everything better—so much better," he gripes. "What good's that going to do when it's already too dark to see in there?"

"Just trust me, brother. You can do this. Just grab ahold of my shirt."

"It ain't going to happen—job waiting on me or not! It just ain't happening! Nobody ever told me that there's a stupid tunnel like this down here. You can say what you want, but I'm not going in there. I'm going to turn around and go back home."

By now, I am finding myself feeling a little bit aggravated with Cecil. There is no way I am letting him chicken out and go back home. I don't care if I have to make him mad at me, and I don't care if he wants to fight me, but I'm going to make him get through this tunnel.

"Daggone it, Cecil, there isn't no way I'm going to let you turn around and go back home and throw this all away. You are going to have to be brave and face your fears. If you don't face your fears, sooner or later you'll be a slave to them for the rest of your life."

Cecil's face flushes red with anger, and he blurts, "Sure, that's easy for you to say when you ain't never been through nothing in your life like I have."

"What's that supposed to mean? We've pretty much been around each other our whole lives, and what one of us has been through, the other one of us was always right there going through it at the same time."

"Yeah, but there are also things you know nothing about that I've been through, things that happened when we were little and you was too young to be running around everywhere like we do now."

A tear trails down Cecil's face, leaving a clean path on his dusty cheek. He wipes his cheek with his hand and sniffs before tilting his head and studying his feet.

"Things like what?" I ask.

"Things like I ain't telling, because it's none of your business."

"All right, then," I say, with a hint of anger and frustration now making its way into my vocal cords. "Don't tell me if you don't want to. But I'm sure, whatever it is, it doesn't have a thing to do with not being able to take a five-minute walk through a stupid tunnel."

"You're dead wrong. It has everything to do with it. Absolutely everything!"

"Okay. Then, if what you are saying is true, why don't you just tell me? Or would you rather me just go around for the rest of my life thinking you're acting like a big baby for no reason?"

I cannot believe that I just accused my big brother of acting like a big baby and he hasn't tried to hit me.

He kicks the pavement, sniffs, and looks at me, his expression so serious I don't know what to say. "Okay," he says. "I'll tell ya, but you better never tell a soul. You better never even speak of it."

"I won't say a word—promise not to."

"Well, when I was about seven, and you were around four or five, when you were too young to remember, I got locked in the outhouse, the old one in the backyard at Mom and Dad's house."

"Locked in the outhouse? What do you mean?"

"I know you don't remember, but when we were kids, we didn't have no indoor plumbing. We had to go outside and do our business, you know, in the johnny house, the one that sets way behind the house that's nailed shut now."

"So what you're saying is getting locked in that johnny house made you claustrophobic?"

"Well, that's just part of it, but that ain't all that happened. You have got to keep in mind that I was only seven years old. Anyway, I went out late one night to use it, an somebody locked me in there—at the time I didn't know who it was. But anyhow, I was just a kid, you know, and it scared the crap out of me. I was screaming and yelling, beating on the walls, and everything. I was going crazy, but he wouldn't let me out. It was a terrible feeling, and to this day, I still remember how it felt.

"But after being trapped in there for so long, I plum freaked out—you know, panicked. I even tried kicking the walls down to get out, and when that didn't work, I got up on the toilet bench to try an knock the ceiling out. But when I got up there, I fell down the hole where all the crap is. And I was trapped down there till Dad and Uncle Tibbs found me and got me out. I was up to my ears in crap and scared out of my mind—thought I was going to die."

I cannot believe my ears, and I find myself feeling terrible about what has happened to my big brother. "Who locked you in there?"

"It was a man they called Sabie Brown—one of the townsfolks."

"Sabie Brown? I've never heard that name before. Why did he do it?"

"Yeah, you've never heard of him because he's been gone a while. But I ain't sure why he done it."

"But how did you know it was him?"

"'Cause Dad and Uncle Tibbs caught him hanging out in the edge of the woods after they rescued me from the crap hole. When they found him, he was laughing like a madman about what he'd done."

"What did they do to him? I'll bet Dad and Tibbs let him have it, didn't they?"

"I don't remember what all happened, but it wasn't good."

"What do you mean, 'it wasn't good'?"

"Well, you've never met Sabie Brown, have ya?"

"What are you trying to say?"

"What I'm trying to say is that Sabie Brown is buried in the mountains out behind our house."

"Yeah, right; you can't be serious."

"Wished I wasn't, but Mom had me out back, and she was drawing water an' cleaning all the poop off me when it happened. They were cussing and a-yelling, and then a fight broke out. Next thing you know, ever'body was crying, and I seen Dad and Uncle Tibbs dragging Sabie by his ankles, talking about they were going to have to bury him."

"Oh no! Tibbs and Dad killed him?"

Cecil breaks out in tears. "I'm sorry. I never wanted to tell you. But they did. They killed him—splattered his brains all over the hillside. I don't want to talk about it no more—just don't ever say a word. Mom said if I ever said anything about it, Dad and Uncle Tibbs would get put away forever."

"Oh man, Cecil. I can't believe I never knew of this. Why'd nobody ever tell me? It isn't any wonder how you came to be so messed up in the head."

"I just don't want to talk about it no more. I just want to forget it, but every time I get these crazy fears, it reminds me all over again. I just hate the feeling that I'm going to be trapped."

"I understand. I understand. I won't talk about it."

It gives me a creepy, yet indescribable feeling to think that my dad and Uncle Tibbs killed a man, buried him, and have been keeping it a secret all these years. I feel so confused about it, and I don't know whether to laugh, cry, pray, be angry, or just try to forget about it. But I guess, for now, I just need to stay focused on getting Cecil through this tunnel.

"I'm sorry about what happened," I say. "But if you ever want to forget about it, you're going to have to face your fears. You know we have to make it to Griggs Town to work, right?"

"Yeah, that's the reason we came here, I reckon."

"Well, the only way we are going to make it to work is by going through this tunnel, and you know that there isn't any other way."

"But what about going over the mountain? Can't we just climb up and go over it instead of going through it?"

"You know as well as I do that ain't going to work. If you try climbing that cliff and going over top of the tunnel, you'll end up getting yourself hurt or even killed."

Cecil sniffs again, wipes away another tear, and goes back to staring at the ground. "Yeah, I know."

"Okay, then. You're going to have to trust me on this one. Grab my shirttail and follow me. We'll be in and out in no time."

Cecil agrees, clutches my shirttail with his strong hand, and follows me into the tunnel. We get about a hundred yards or more inside, and there is still no sign of daylight on the other end. I'm expecting him to freak out at any second, but so far, he seems to be handling it well.

And after traveling another hundred yards or so, the glow of the light from the tunnel's entrance fades, and darkness consumes us. Cecil's breathing gets faster, and he pushes me to pick up the pace. "It's all right, Cecil. Just hang in there, and I promise you that feeling will go away. Slow your breathing and take slow, deep breaths. There is nothing that's going to hurt you. It's all in your mind."

As we descend deeper into the tunnel, Cecil releases my shirt. "You know, it's not that bad," he says. "I freaked out for a little bit, but after a few minutes those feelings started going away. I reckon you are right—if I just face 'em, they'll go away."

"It's true. I've read about it before. They say if you face your fear over and over again, no matter what it is you're afraid of, you will eventually overcome it."

"You're a book-reading maniac, aren't you? But I guess all that reading you've done was good for something."

"Ha, I suppose it was. But look, there's finally some light at the end of the tunnel. We're almost there."

"It's about time. This tunnel must be a mile long."

"Yeah, if not more. And look at the bright side; you faced your fear, and you made it."

"Yeah, and it feels good, I reckon. But I also reckon I had you going pretty good back there, didn't I?"

"What do you mean?"

"You know what I mean. Dad and Tibbs didn't really kill anybody. You didn't actually believe me, did ya? You know Dad and Uncle Tibbs wouldn't hurt a fly."

"They didn't? You mean they didn't kill him, and you made all that stupid stuff up?"

"Well, I didn't make it *all* up, just the part about Sabie Brown—Sabie Brown never existed. But everything else happened. I did get locked in the johnny house, and I did fall down the crap hole."

"Okay, so if there was no Sabie Brown, how did you get locked in there?"

"Well, the truth is, the wind blew the door shut on the johnny, and the lever—I mean, latch or whatever you call it—fell or slid down and locked the door. I was just a kid an freaked out, you know?"

"Daggone it, Cecil, why did you have to say all that crap about Dad and Uncle Tibbs? You even went as far as to shed tears when you were telling it."

"I don't know. But I suppose I just got carried away. I reckon I figured if I had a real good story about how I got claustrophobic, you wouldn't give me such a hard time and I wouldn't have to kick your hind end over it. You got to admit, though, it was an awful good story."

"No! As a matter of fact, it was a terrible story. It was wrong—just wrong. I can't believe that you did that to me. You had me upset over it all. But I'm glad that it wasn't true. I got the creeps something awful about it; thinking Dad and Tibbs had killed somebody was awful. But now that we are being honest, I suppose that I have something to tell you."

13

'm not sure you can top that," Cecil says, "but let's hear it—give it a shot."

"Well, I'm not trying to compete with you, but do you remember when you woke up yesterday with your foot on fire?"

"Umm, yeah…" He pauses, stares at me suspiciously, and says, "How could I forget?"

"Well, the truth about that is it was my fault. I got up early, before you woke up, and I raked those hot coals next to your foot and blew on the coals a bit to get them going. Then I hurried back over to lie down so you wouldn't think it was me."

"You sneaky good-for-nothing—you burnt the sole off my shoe! I'm going to knock you a good one over that!"

Cecil reaches over to grab me, so I take off running, and he chases me the rest of the way out of the tunnel. He catches up to me and smacks me on the back of the head. "Okay, you sneaky little turd," he says. "We're even now. You pull something like that again, and next time it will be a fist upside your head."

"All right, all right, Cecil, let's just knock it off. There are houses all around, and people can see us. We'd better stop horsing around and start acting normal before we draw any unwanted attention."

For reasons I don't understand, a feeling of intimidation grips my soul, as I observe the beautiful homes that stand among manicured lawns and mulch-smothered flower beds. I feel a bit out of place in this wealthy atmosphere with my dirty face, worn-out clothes, and ragged shoes, but I suppose there isn't anything I can do except try not to think about it. Maybe it will make me feel better if I can find a place to change my clothes and wash myself up a little.

After what feels like about five more miles of walking, we cross a small bridge that extends over a narrow creek. To our right we see what appears to be the Griggs Town water reservoir that S's newspaper article mentioned. Scattered all around the edges of the water are cedar-sided shops, a board-and-batten-sided church with a large cross on the top of its steeple, and several other wood-sided buildings. Everything is stained and painted up. It's a beautiful place.

We skip down the bank and under the bridge to clean ourselves up near the water. I empty my sack to find a decent pair of pants, but I soon realize that doing so is going to be an impossible task. I have no decent pants. All my pants have holes and grass stains, but I guess the pair with the smallest holes and fewest stains will have to be good enough. Being in such a fancy place as this has me feeling shameful about how worn-out they look, but at least I am not alone in the shame. Cecil's pants are as worn-out as mine.

We clean up the best we can by using our bare hands to splash the creek water on our faces and scrub the dirt off our arms and elbows. I watch as the dark water that drips from my face and arms dilutes in the stream. Cecil dunks his head in the creek and gives his dirty hair a quick scrub; for the sake of getting the smell of sweat off me, I decide to do the same.

We get halfway cleaned up and into a fresh change of clothes and decide that we should go ahead and see if we can find the mine before checking out the town. When we leave the creek bank and get back on the road, a friendly, well-dressed man riding a bicycle stops, makes short conversation, welcomes us to town, and points us in the direction of the mine. After a short ten- to fifteen-minute walk past the reservoir, we find this awful-looking place that lacks the beauty we've seen in Griggs thus far. There is no sign to tell us what this place is, but based on the large stone cliffs, the sounds of heavy equipment, and the sight of an endless cloud of dust, we gather that we have finally arrived at the Swift silver mine.

A twenty-foot-high wall made of gray, edge-rusted corrugated steel rises from the ground. It stretches from a stone-faced cliff a few hundred yards to the left of me and extends as far as the eye can see to my right. A guard booth constructed of the same corrugated material sits next to a large chain-driven gate that looks to be the sole entrance to the mine.

As we get closer, two men exit the booth, tapping the pistols that dangle from their waists in worn leather holsters. The taller of the two, a man with greasy black hair, black-framed glasses, and patchy facial hair, clears his throat and says, "You boys need to make a U-turn and head back to wherever you've come from—there won't be no hanging around here."

The greasy-haired man points up the road and nudges his short, hairless partner with his sharp elbow. His partner snickers and says, "You heard the man. Now turn around and head back from whence you came."

As I expect, Cecil's face flushes red with anger, and he starts running his mouth. "Now, you just wait a minute. If this is the Swift silver mine, we got every right to be here. Is it or not?"

"It is," the greasy-haired man says. "But that don't give you no right to be here. Now, move on."

Cecil takes two steps toward the man and says, "I won't be moving anywhere. You can come and try to move me if you want, but me and my brother here are going to be working in this mine."

"That's funny you would say that," the man says as he switches from tapping his pistol to rubbing it, "'cause they ain't hiring."

"Now wait a minute," I say. "I talked to a man named Mr. Slusher a few days ago, and he told us that we have a job. You had better get on your radio and find him. We didn't come all this way for nothing."

"Tough luck," the greasy-headed man proclaims. "I guess that spells bad news for you two. There isn't no Mr. Slusher that works here. Ain't that right, Geraldine?"

He nudges the hairless man again with his elbow, encouraging him to agree. "That's right. They ain't no Mr. Slusher."

ecil takes a few more steps forward. "I'll be doggone!" Cecil shouts. "I've had to sleep in ditches, almost starve to death, and walk for miles and miles just to make it here, so you sure as heck best be finding me a Mr. Slusher somewhere. And if he ain't here, you best be telling me where I can find him."

The two men smirk but don't respond, so Cecil continues. "Oh, so you two think it's funny, do you?" And before I can even try to talk Cecil out of it, he charges over and doesn't stop until he's standing almost on top of them. "Answer me!" he demands.

The men scramble to pull the pistols from their holsters. "You might as well go ahead and pull that trigger and shoot me now," Cecil says, "because if one of you don't answer me real quick, I'm going to kick both of you in the dirt."

The tall man's eyes get as greasy as his head, and he seems to be intimidated by Cecil's presence as he takes a few steps back. "Hey, just calm down and take it easy. Relax," he says. "We're just screwing around with you. Can't nobody take a joke anymore?" He turns and snaps at the short, hairless man, "Geraldine, get on the radio and get them an escort to Mr. Slusher."

Geraldine smashes the button on his handheld radio. And within seconds, an older man wearing gray coveralls, a hard hat, and safety glasses meets us at the gate. He pulls a clipboard from beneath his armpit. After requesting our names and being satisfied that he finds our names on the list, he hands us each a hard hat, leads us behind the corrugated wall and up a flight of steel steps, then leaves us at the door of Mr. Slusher's office.

I'm thinking now that we should have stashed our dirty feed sacks somewhere before coming in here, but it's a little too late for that now. I hope he doesn't ask us what we're doing with them.

I get nervous as I enter the office, but Mr. Slusher puts me at ease with a warm smile and a firm handshake. "You two must be the Pochaw brothers, Cecil and Greenway."

"Yes, sir," I say.

"Yes," Cecil adds.

He eyes our pig-feed bags for a few seconds but doesn't say anything about them. "Pleased to meet you, I'm Bodie Slusher," he says.

"It's a pleasure to meet you, too," I say. "My name is Greenway."

I glance over at Cecil, and I'm half worried that he will say something stupid, but he smiles like a gentleman and says, "Hi, it's a pleasure to meet you. My name is Cecil Pochaw."

"I'm sure glad you made it. Will you be ready to start work in the morning?"

"Yes sir," I say as Cecil nods his head in agreement.

"Good. Good. I have some paperwork for you two to fill out, but since we're about ready to shut down for the day, you can just fill it out in the morning. Why don't you two follow me, and I'll show you where you'll be working."

Mr. Slusher escorts us out of his office and down the steps. Cecil and I stare at each other in confusion as he leads us back toward the front gate. He punches a combination into an electronic keypad that works the gate and says in a whisper, "You boys need to remember this. I just changed the code on this thing." He pulls an ink pen and a piece of paper from his shirt pocket and hands it to me. "Here you go, write this down: One-nine-zero-two. You got it?"

"Yes," I say, expecting his next line of instruction.

"All right, now enter those numbers on the box and hit the star key."

I do as he says, and the gate rolls open. "Good," he says. "Now, keep those numbers in a safe place, and whatever you do, don't lose them. Just the three of us have these numbers, so let's keep it that way. Now follow me." Mr. Slusher leads us through the open gate and takes us around to where Geraldine and the tall, greasy-headed man are sitting in the guard booth.

Mr. Slusher shifts his gentle facial expressions to something more serious as he approaches the two men. "You are fired," he says. "Hand over your pistols and your radios. Your final checks will be in the mail."

The men deal us an evil stare as if we are somehow responsible for Mr. Slusher's actions. A bead of sweat, or maybe even grease, boils up and drips from the greasy-headed man's brow. "Firing us for doing what?" he gripes, then spits on the ground in my direction. "Them boys is lying, because me and Geraldine ain't done nothing wrong."

"They didn't say you did, but I can bet you two gave them a rough way to go, just like you do everyone else who comes through here. I got three complaints today before it was even lunchtime. And I told you two long ago that if you kept it up, you were going to get fired. Needless to say, these men standing here with me today will be serving as your replacements." Mr. Slusher glances at us and grins.

The two men slam down their pistols and radios onto a table inside the guard booth. Geraldine reaches over to a stack of file folders filled with papers, grabs it, and slings the lot of them toward Cecil and me. But the papers fly out of the folders and rock back and forth in the air until they fall to the ground, never reaching our feet.

Mr. Slusher charges over to the guard booth and gets right in their faces. "You get out of here right this second," Mr. Slusher demands.

The tall man swipes his forearm across his greasy forehead and adds, "Yeah, we'll go all right, but you just wait till I catch you two boys out somewhere. You'll be sorry you ever crossed my path."

And to my surprise, Cecil stays calm and offers the two men a smile as they charge away, cursing random phrases. Mr. Slusher grins, shrugs his shoulders, and scratches his head of messy gray hair. "I tell you what. Those two guys right there beat all I've ever seen, and I am glad to see them go. I don't expect you two bright young men would ever behave in such a manner while working here."

"No, sir," I say.

"You never have to worry about that," Cecil adds.

"Well, now that that's over with," Mr. Slusher says, "it's down to business. Your starting pay here will be ten an hour. You are to be here from seven in the morning until six in the evening— Monday through Friday. You get an hour for lunch—twelve till one. Payday will be every other week, and I'll have you in our payroll system by noon tomorrow, so you'll get your first check, not this coming Friday, but on the following Friday. Your guns and radios are to be locked in the guard booth every evening, and the code I just gave you to open the gate will be the same code you use to get into the guard booth. Any questions?"

"Yes," Cecil says. "What is it we are supposed to be doing?"

"Don't worry about that, just be here at 7:00 a.m., and I will send somebody down to help you through your first day."

We lock the guns and radios up in the guard booth and head to town.

"I can't believe it," Cecil says as we start walking away. "Did that really just happen back there?"

"I don't know. It almost sounds too good to be true, doesn't it? Did he really just say that we're getting ten an hour?"

"That's what he said," Cecil says with a laugh. "And to top it off, it looks like we'll be running the guard booth and slinging pistols all day to make that money."

"That's what I thought he said, but I was afraid I might have heard him wrong. I had been hoping the whole time that he would offer us at least five an hour, but I never would have guessed that we'd end up getting this much. We'll be rich in a day's time at this rate! Nobody back home is going to believe it. Nobody! And I can't believe that he just handed us the code to the gate."

"Tell me about it, Greenway. Dad and Tibbs aren't going to believe it when they hear we are just about running the place."

"Well, let's go see if we can find an envelope and a stamp somewhere, so we can tell everybody the news. We have to send a letter, anyway, to tell Mom and Auntie Rose about that money we hid for them in the barn."

We find an old general store in town that sells almost everything. With our last little bit of change, we purchase a stamped envelope and drop a letter to our folks in the mail. "I can't wait till they get it," Cecil says. "I'll bet they'll be packed up and here in a week once they open that."

"I don't know about that. I think it will take a lot more than a letter to prove anything to Dad and Tibbs. You know how they are."

"Well, I guess it doesn't matter all that much what they think. All I care is that we get to make some real money."

Cecil and I find a full patch of grass next to the blue-green tinted reservoir and drop down to relax. For a moment, everything seems perfect, and I can't imagine anything being capable of removing this smile from my face. But no sooner does this sense of relief set in than I realize we have a major problem.

Cecil stares me down as the smile on my face dissipates. "What the crap is the matter now?" he asks. "You look like you're getting sick or something."

"Well, I don't know. After all we've been through so far, I should just be able to laugh about it."

"Laugh about what?"

"Well, brother, I'll put it to you like this. We're supposed to be at work tomorrow morning at seven, right?"

"That's what he told us."

"Okay, what time is it now?"

"Now that's a stupid question. S stole our watch. You know that. I don't have a watch."

"Yeah, and I don't have a watch, either."

A confused look seems to occupy Cecil's face, but then his mouth drops open, and his eyes widen. "Oh no," he says. "I see what you mean. How in the world are we supposed to hold down a job when we ain't got a clue to what time o' day it is? We have to figure something out, or we are going to be late and get canned on the first day."

"I don't know. We can buy a watch at the end of next week when we get paid, but until then we're going to have to think of something."

"Yeah, and it better be quick. Mr. Slusher done fired them guys—done it right in front of us. And if we ain't there on time in the morning, we'll get fired."

"I know what we can do, Cecil. Let's just go sleep by the guard booth, and when all the folks start showing up to work in the morning, that should wake us."

"That's not a bad idea at all, Greenway. That's pretty smart. They might catch us snoozing, but at least we will be there on time, and they won't fire us for that."

We sit by the reservoir and eat the last of our potted meat and crackers for supper, then we relax for the rest of the evening. And when the sun begins to set, we make our way back to the mine. Using our feed sacks as pillows, we lie down beside the guard booth and fall asleep.

15

The next morning, the sound of a car door slamming wakes us, and we jump to our feet and stand beside the guard booth. "Good morning, men," Mr. Slusher says as he approaches us in the dim morning light. He glances down at his watch. "It's not yet six o'clock, and you're here an hour early."

I stumble to speak, unsure how to answer, but finally manage to say, "We just didn't want to be late."

Mr. Slusher grins and says, "I don't know quite what to say, but in my ten years of running this place, I've never had anyone show up for work an hour early . . . maybe an hour late, but never early. I thought that the good old-fashioned work ethic was a thing of the past."

"Well, sir," Cecil says, "this is the best opportunity we've ever had, and we don't want to ruin it."

There is an awkward moment of silence while Mr. Slusher appears to be at a loss for words. I try to think of a reasonable way to respond and break the silence, but I can't put my jumbled thoughts into words. I am relieved as a smile stretches across Mr. Slusher's face, and he breaks the silence. "You know what?" he says. "I have a good feeling about you two, and I think that ten dollars an hour won't be enough as starting pay. I think I'm going to bump you up to eleven an hour. Any objections to that?"

"No, sir," I say. "No objections at all!"

I look over at Cecil and, just as I would expect, I see him grinning from ear to ear. He looks at Mr. Slusher and says, "Of course not. There will be no objections to that, whatsoever. You can pay us as much as you want."

"All right, then," Mr. Slusher says. "We'll consider it done. And by the way, let's just keep this between us, if you don't mind."

For the rest of the day, with the help of a kind man named Mr. Pink, who was appointed by Mr. Slusher, Cecil and I learn all about gun safety, talking on handheld radios, and opening the front gate, which seem to be the only major tasks required to perform our new job. It's hard to believe that we are going to be getting paid to do this. But it's tough to feel too excited about things on such an empty stomach. We've had no breakfast and no lunch because we are all out of food and money, and I don't know how in the world we are going to survive until we get our first paycheck.

After our first day of work comes to an end, we dash into town, hoping that we can find something to eat. I'm so hungry that I am willing to eat out of a trash can. But I quickly realize that doing this is out of the question, as there are too many people around. I am desperate, but not desperate enough to earn a bad reputation from it.

We see the bridge under which we washed ourselves up and changed our clothes the previous day, and we rush down to the bank to see if we can find any fish in the creek. We can't. We pause for a moment, unsure of what to do next. Then Cecil glances at me with a serious expression and says, "Don't even think about it."

"Think about what?"

"Think about eating bugs again. Don't even think about it. Let's just sit here for a minute and come up with a plan." He plops down and sits in the tan-colored dirt that lines the edge of the creek for as far as the eye can see. A look of discouragement fills his eyes, and he says, "Maybe we can just ask for some food. Have you ever thought about that?"

"Ask who?" I say. "We sure can't ask anything from the townspeople. You and I know that the second we do, everybody will be treating us like bums, just like they all did at Mr. Jenny's store, and we'll never hear the end of it. The only person I'll ever ask anything from again is God."

Cecil looks at me with an aggravated look on his face and says, "Well, then, ask God, why don't you?"

"I done did it," I say. "I asked Him all day about it."

"Well, now what? I'm starving."

"I don't know," I say. "I guess we will just have to wait until the town shuts down and then go look in the trash cans or the dumpsters. There might be something behind one of the stores. If there is a grocery store, you know there is almost always out-of-date stuff or old fruit and vegetables they throw out."

As soon as the words leave my lips, a feeling of defeat washes over me, and the hunger pains in my stomach seem to deepen. But I am immediately distracted by the sound of footsteps and voices coming from the bridge above us, followed by the sound of something hitting the ground and splashing in the water behind us. I turn around to investigate and see small white chunks of something floating in the water, as well as lying on the bank of the creek. While I am observing this, more chunks rain down from above.

Cecil also turns around and whispers, "What in the world is going on?" He gets up, walks to a white chunk, and bends over to pick it up. As soon as he does so, a large goose emerges from the vegetation and charges at him, hissing. Cecil screams and takes off running. Naturally, I follow. As we reach the top of the bank, we are met with laughter coming from two older men. After chuckling together over Cecil's girlish squeal, we learn that the men are bakers from the bakery next door. They tell us that they bring out all the old bread every evening to feed the ducks, geese, and other waterfowl. But little did they know they were about to have a few more guests for supper.

As soon as the men finish tossing the rest of their bread over the bridge and return to their bakery, we return to the creek and manage to salvage several large chunks of bread from the ground as well as the branches of the nearby bushes. This time we stand our ground, unintimidated by the grouchy geese, while we fill our stomachs with several different varieties of bread, including what I assume to be banana bread, or at least what I hope is banana bread.

And so, for the next week and a half, Cecil and I sleep, wake, and enjoy working at the security booth, and at night literally break bread with the geese, ducks, and other birds. Finally, Mr. Slusher meets us at the guard booth with our first paycheck. We sprint all the way to the bank, and I gasp as the bank teller counts out several hundred dollars for me. There is so much money in my hand that I can feel the weight of it.

"Whoa, I'm rich," Cecil says with a laugh as the teller drops the money in his hand. The teller grins and rolls her eyes.

We leave the bank in shock over the amount of money that we have just put in our pockets. And without even discussing it, we hide our pig feed bags in the bushes and stop at the first restaurant we see: the Clapboard Pancake House. Cecil yanks the door open and leads the way inside. A beautiful lady with wavy red hair, wearing a knee-length navy-blue apron, greets us at the end of a short hallway. "How many?" she asks.

Cecil shoots her the funniest-looking stare that I have ever seen and says, "I'll take a whole stack of pancakes and a whole side of bacon, if you don't mind." The lady blushes and giggles. "What's so funny?" Cecil asks, and before he even allows her to answer, he continues, "Well, I guess it's a lot, but I'm hungry." The lady giggles again.

"Hold on just a minute," she says. "I was asking how many, as in how many of you need a table."

"Oh, I see," Cecil says. "There are just two of us—my brother and me—but if you want to join us, you can."

She smiles politely and says, "I'm working, so I guess you two will have to get along without me. Follow me. I'll find you a table, and your waitress will be right with you."

We place our order with the waitress, and a few minutes later we are up to our elbows in pancake syrup and bacon grease. When I am nearly finished with my double-stack of pancakes, I look up and notice two beautiful girls sitting at a table across the aisle, staring at us. Embarrassed, I stop stuffing my face and kick Cecil to let him know that we are being watched. He smiles at the girls and waves at them—with two half-eaten strips of bacon still stuffed between his fingers. He then turns back toward his plate and continues to shovel food into his mouth.

I look down, hoping that their attention will focus elsewhere, but when I look back up, they seem to be staring even harder at us. Any other time, I would be excited to have beautiful girls paying attention to me, but I have this terrible feeling that they only notice us because we are currently looking and acting like two filthy hogs.

Fortunately, the waitress comes by their table to drop off their check, and I am relieved as they pay and get up to leave.

As soon as they are gone, I go back to stuffing my face. Just as I am getting carried away with my meal—and when I say carried away, I mean having a mouth overstuffed with food, while holding a forkful of eggs in one hand and a fistful of bacon in the other—someone taps me on the shoulder. A soft female voice floats through the air behind me. "Would it be okay if we joined you for a minute?"

While visualizing myself covered with pig fat from head to toe, I empty my hands and turn around to see the owner of the sweet voice. To my surprise, I see that the two beautiful girls who had been sitting across from us are now standing behind us. As any decent human being would do, I invite them to sit down.

The girl with sandy blonde hair halfway down her neck and eyes as blue and clear as the summer sky pulls out a chair and sits down beside me. The other girl, whose beauty is less intimidating, but still attractive—auburn hair and emerald-green eyes—sits down across from me next to Cecil.

"My name is Cass," the girl sitting beside me says.

"And my name is Janie," the other girl says.

For a moment, Cecil and I are dumbstruck and don't say anything, so Cass takes it upon herself to carry the conversation. "Don't you all have names?"

"Oh, I apologize," I say. "My name is Greenway."

We all focus our attention on Cecil as he finishes chomping a mouthful of bacon. "Sorry, I'm hungry. My name's Cecil, but my friends call me—well, I guess everybody just calls me Cecil." He extends his greasy palm, shakes their hands, and then continues to shovel another load of bacon into his mouth. The girls smile and grab a napkin from the table to wipe the grease off their hands.

"Sorry about that," Cecil says, as half-chewed bacon bounces between his front teeth and his lips. "It has been a long time since I had any bacon—a good month or more."

Cass twists her chair slightly and looks at me, insisting that I make eye contact with her. "So, Greenway," she says. "You and your friend here must think we're crazy, don't you?"

"Oh, he's not my friend; he's my brother. And why would we think you're crazy?" I ask, confused by her question. It seems to me that we are the ones who look crazy, covered in pancake crumbs and bacon drippings.

"I don't know," she answers with a hint of shyness, unable to hold the eye contact that she demanded of me. "I was just afraid that you would think we're crazy for asking to sit down. Janie said you would think that we are nuts if we came over here."

Before I can even respond, Cecil interrupts. "Now wait a minute—you two ain't prostitutes, are you?"

The girls' mouths drop open, so I jump in to try to smooth things over. "Shut up, Cecil," I say, putting all the pleading I can in the look I give him, "Don't pay no mind to my brother," I say to the girls. "He's just kidding."

"I sure ain't kidding!" Cecil barks, looking as ridiculous as ever with bacon grease smeared across his cheeks. "The last time we had a pretty woman come over and start talking all nice to us, she tried to take our money and get us in trouble with the law."

I am envisioning either Cecil getting slapped in the face or the girls getting up and storming out of the restaurant. But to my surprise, Cass and Janie just look at each other and giggle. "In your dreams," Janie says, before joining Cass in another round of giggling.

Cass stands up and instructs Janie to do the same. "You guys are funny. But we will let you finish your breakfast. Janie and I will be sitting out front by the water, so if you want to talk, you know where to find us." Without saying another word, Cass grabs Janie's hand and leads her out of the restaurant.

Cecil hurries to finish off his last corner of pancakes and says, "You go ahead and finish eating. I'm going to run out there and keep them girls company 'fore they run off."

"Can't you please just wait until I'm done?" I say, not wanting to finish my breakfast alone.

"There ain't no way, Greenway. Those girls are pretty, and you eat as slow as Grandma." And so, without further discussion, Cecil takes off out the door and leaves me to finish eating all on my own.

16

As soon as I am finished, I hurry outside and notice Cass, Janie, and Cecil sitting cross-legged on a short pier that extends out into the reservoir. When I approach, I find them engaged in uncontrolled laughter. I drop down to sit beside Cass and learn that Cecil had just shared the prostitute story. After about an hour's worth of stories inspired by Cecil's warped sense of humor, Cass and I break away into our own conversation, forcing Janie and Cecil to do the same. For the next little bit, we talk about everything from where we were born to subjects as ridiculous as our favorite color. And before the light of the evening fades, Cass and Janie lead us to a nearby inn to help us find a room to rent.

Cass and Janie introduce us to the innkeeper, a kind older lady related to Janie, who offers us a space where we can stay as long as we like, for the weekly rate of $77 each. That seems expensive to me, but with the amount of money that we will be making it shouldn't be a problem.

The girls help us find the door to our room and give each of us a friendly hug before saying goodnight and leaving us standing there.

Cecil looks at me and smiles and says, "Did you see that, Greenway? Janie just hugged me. I think she likes me. I think she really does."

"There is no doubt she likes you," I say. "Can you please just unlock the door so we can see our room? I would love a shower."

"I would, but I'm waiting on you. I ain't got no key."

"They didn't give me the key; I thought you had it."

"No, they didn't give me one. I seen her hand it to you."

"All she gave me was this card."

"Yeah, Greenway, that's because it's a *key* card. She said you have to insert it into the slot to get in. Weren't you listening? Here, give me the card." Cecil yanks the card from my hand, stabs it into the brass slot below the doorknob and opens the door. "See, Greenway? You couldn't make it in this world without your big bro."

Cecil walks in before me and fumbles for the light switch. "Oh, my goodness, Greenway. This ain't no room. It's a doggone mansion!"

I peer into the room with amazement. "There is no way that this is our room," I say. "This has to be some kind of mistake."

"This ain't a mistake. Do you see what it says on the door? It says number forty-five, just like the lady at the front desk said. It's even written on the key card."

"Wow, this is unreal, Cecil. This is going to take some getting used to."

Shiny white tiles with thin veins of silver and black serve as the flooring at the entryway, merging with dark walnut flooring that covers the rest of the space. A large bathroom occupies the entire corner of the room, housing a large bathtub and a walk-in shower, each lined to the ceiling with dark marble tiles, while a full kitchen occupies the opposite corner. Three arched windows and two double sliding-glass doors make up the far wall, leading to a second-story balcony that offers an elevated view of the water reservoir. A sitting area, consisting of two brown leather chairs and a round coffee table, is situated over a thick maroon rug, lying in front of the large balcony doors. And lastly, two bedrooms with soft queen-sized beds and TVs occupy the rest of the space. Clearly, no expense was spared when they built this place.

After finishing my first real shower in roughly two weeks, I slide into my soft bed and flip through the TV channels until I fall to sleep.

The following morning, I am woken up by a knock at the door. I rush over to open it and find, to my surprise, Cass and Janie standing there, hugging paper grocery bags and talking about how they are going to make Cecil and me breakfast. "What in the world is going on in here?" Cecil asks as he walks through the hallway, stretching and yawning, wearing nothing but a pair of solid white underwear. "Something ain't right here. I reckon I'm still dreaming. But if I'm dreaming, whatever you do, please don't wake me."

"You're not dreaming," Janie says.

Cecil looks down and realizes he is wearing nothing but his underwear and rushes out of the room. Cass and Janie walk over and set their brown grocery bags on the kitchen counter. Cecil returns a minute later, wearing clothing.

Cass walks over and puts her arms around my neck and looks me in the eyes. "I thought about you most of the night," she says. "Won't you have a seat and relax? I'll make you a cup of coffee, and then we are going to make you all some breakfast—that is, if you don't mind."

I just look at her and grin. She knows that I don't mind.

As Cecil and I sip hot coffee, the girls heat up the stove eyes and begin cooking us breakfast. It looks like we're going to have a little bit of everything: sausage links, bacon, eggs, and even biscuits and gravy.

I've never felt so well-to-do in my life. I have a pocketful of money, a fancy place to rest at night, and a beautiful girl who can cook. I couldn't ask for anything more at this moment. I had a feeling that things would be better in Griggs Town, but I never imagined all this. If only Dad and Uncle Tibbs could see me now . . . if only.

After Cecil and I eat more than any two men should, the girls take us out to spend the day on the town. They drag us through nearly every shop, store, and building, one in which I am finally able to purchase a watch. They also introduce us to some of the nicest folks we've ever met. We even get to meet this one old man whom the townspeople call "Pajamas." Cass and Janie say that he's an escapee from the old folks home. They say he escapes at least twice a week, and they always find him by the reservoir sitting in his white flannel pajamas and holding a homemade fishing pole. They claim he is crazy, but I don't see it. It seems to me that the man just likes to fish. I suppose I'd be doing the same thing if I were in his shoes—or, in this case, his pajamas.

By the time five o'clock rolls around, I feel as if I have shaken more hands in a day than an average politician manages to shake in a week. The girls suspect we are tired and hungry after this friendly campaign, and they offer to purchase some sandwiches and bottled sodas from the diner for all of us to enjoy. After they refuse our offer to pay, we take the food and relax on the bank of the reservoir for a picnic.

After we finish eating, Cecil and Janie walk off to the other side of the bank, while Cass and I continue to lie on the ground and talk as the sun begins to set. Cass is on her side with her head propped up by her hand, just staring at me and smiling so sweetly. While I talk, she appears to absorb every word I say, as if I matter to her. I'm not sure why such a beautiful girl would want anything to do with a hillbilly like me, because nobody has *ever* wanted me. But it sure feels good, just the same.

Cecil and Janie, on the other hand, don't appear to be sharing the same magical moment. All I can hear coming from them is excessive talking and giggling. At one point I even hear a loud fart followed by uncontrollable laughter.

But before the light of the day completely fades, the girls tell us they have somewhere to be with their families and bid us goodnight. I'm a bit disappointed that they have to call it a night already, but at least they don't say goodbye without promising to swing by for another breakfast before walking with us to church tomorrow morning.

———

It is Sunday morning, ten minutes before church service is set to start, and Cass and Janie still haven't shown up. Cecil is ranting, "Where the heck are they? I just don't get it. Everything seemed so perfect. I should have known better than to trust a stupid girl. If they think I'm waiting on them around here all day, they are going to find out different. I don't need no woman."

After the moment Cass and I shared last night, I'm sure that something important must have come up. So I try to console Cecil. "Just calm down," I say. "I'm sure we'll hear something from them soon; they wouldn't ditch us—especially not church—for no good reason. Something must have come up. You know that."

From the look on Cecil's face, I can see that my attempt to console him has failed. "I don't know anything," he gripes, pouting. "It ain't like we've known them our whole lives or anything. What kind of girl promises you breakfast and then doesn't show up?"

"We can eat something later," I say, sensing that Cecil is mostly thinking with his stomach. "But if we hurry, we can still make it to church on time. If they're running behind, chances are they will just show up there. But just in case they come by here looking for us, we can leave them a note on our door to let them know where we are."

Sadly, the girls never show up while we are at church, and when we return to our room, we see that the note we left on the door hasn't been touched. I thought for sure we would have heard something from them by now. I must admit, I'm starting to feel just as bad as Cecil is about the whole thing. I begin to wonder if I said something I shouldn't have to Cass. Maybe I offended her somehow, and she no longer wants anything to do with me. Or maybe it was Cecil's fault. Maybe he said something crazy when he and Janie were alone talking—he always says the craziest things.

The rest of the day crawls by, and we still don't hear anything from the girls. It gives me this sick feeling, much like the time I felt after drinking spoiled milk. It's almost impossible to recall the feeling of perfection that seemed to saturate every thought of yesterday. I now lie here on my bed, in the most beautiful space I have ever occupied; I have a pocketful of money and a lot to be thankful for, but I still feel miserable. Why did I ever have to meet Cass? I guess I should just try to forget about her and remember why I am here.

The next day at work seems to drag by, and it is difficult to focus on anything other than how the girls ditched us. Cecil hasn't said three words all morning and only seems to find comfort in spinning his revolver on his finger. After growing bored with that, he takes aim at a squirrel through the window of the booth. "I'm going to shoot him. I'll bet you twenty I can hit him in the head."

"Yeah," I say. "You pull that trigger, and Mr. Slusher will be sending us walking, like he did the other two guys that were working here."

Cecil grins crookedly and says, "At this point, I don't even care."

And before I can say another word, Cecil squeezes the trigger. *Click.* It doesn't fire. "What in the world . . . these stupid guns aren't even real," Cecil gripes.

I cannot even believe that he just pulled the trigger. "Cecil, are you crazy? Please stop. You are going to get us fired."

He opens the cylinder of the pistol and dumps the bullets into the palm of his hand and examines them. "Get fired for what? Shooting blanks?" He holds up a single bullet to show me where it was struck with the firing pin. "You see, the stupid thing didn't even go off. That's because they're fake."

"And it's a good thing it didn't go off," I say. "Now please just put the bullets away and stop playing with the gun before you get us fired. I know you're not happy about the girls, and neither am I, but that doesn't mean we should stop caring about our jobs. We just have to try to remember Mom and Auntie Rose and why we came here."

Cecil returns the bullets to the gun's cylinder, resumes spinning it, and says, "I know. I wasn't thinking right. But it's a good thing these bullets ain't real. I knew there was no way that Mr. Slusher would hand us a gun with real bullets in it. These guns are only for show. But you know, I wish them girls never had done us that way. I mean, I wish we'd never met them 'cause I was happy until they came along. And now I just can't seem to think right. It's messing with my head. I thought Janie liked me."

"Well, maybe something happened and they just couldn't make it. I know it probably isn't so, but maybe."

The sad expression on Cecil's face transforms into something more pleasant. "You know," he says, "I reckon I have been acting like a fool all along, because I don't need no woman. And I ain't about to let one control how I feel—especially one that I just met." He smiles, apparently waiting for me to nod my head in agreement, so I do. "I think I'm going to take my chair and go out there and sit in the sun. You want to come?"

I grab my chair and follow him outside. We struggle to position our chairs on the unlevel ground and can't seem to get them to sit straight. "Nothing's working right," he whines. "And I'm tired of screwing with it. I reckon I'll just stand here."

He kicks his chair over, leans up against the guard booth, and starts spinning his gun again. "You know," he says, "I wonder if

Mom and Rose got our letter and found that money we hid for them in the barn?"

"Yeah. I would say they got the letter and found it by now. I'll bet they didn't know what to think about it."

"I'd say you're right, and I'll bet Mom had that Mr. Jenny's panties in a bunch in front of everybody at the store when she pulled out that twenty-dollar bill. He's going to think that we all done got rich."

"I hope so, and I hope he feels bad about himself for treating our family like bums," I say.

Cecil smiles proudly and nods his head. "I'd say so," he says. "But you just wait. When we get off work, I'm going down to the post office and send Mom and them a whole hundred-dollar bill. They sure could use it, and that will definitely get that Mr. Jenny going good this time. I'll bet you he'll cry, trying to make change on a hundred."

And just when I was about to tell him that I would put a hundred in there, too, a black SUV comes speeding into the parking lot, slides through the gravel, and stops about twenty yards in front of us. Two men exit the vehicle. They are dressed in dark suits with belts holding tightly tucked shirts. They rush over to us. "Open the gate and let us in," one of the men demands.

"Sorry, but it ain't quite that easy," Cecil says in a relaxed tone, spinning the pistol carelessly on his finger. "We need to have your reason for being here and radio you in for an escort. Do you have an appointment?"

The men flip the sides of their jackets open, revealing shoulder-harnessed pistols and shiny metal badges dangling from black leather squares. "I'd say we don't require an appointment. We're here looking for the Pochaw brothers, Cecil and Greenway."

"Well, hey, that's us," Cecil says. "What do you want?"

The men step backward and slide their hands in their jackets, appearing to place their hands on their guns. "Toss your guns on the ground," one of the men shouts.

"Hey, hey, just calm down," Cecil says. "These guns are all for show. They're not even real—just watch." Cecil aims his pistol toward the treetops and squeezes the trigger. *Bang!* The gun discharges. "Whoa!" Cecil shouts. "I guess the bullets *are* real." The men run and take cover behind their SUV.

My heart is pounding, and my ears are ringing. "What in the world?!" I cry. "Why didn't you just put the stupid gun down?"

But before he can even answer, the suited men fire off two rounds from their own pistols, which zip past us and pierce the corrugated steel behind us. "The maniac is trying to kill us! Run, Greenway—run!" Cecil takes off toward the woods, and without having much choice, other than death, I follow.

With random gunshots firing behind us, Cecil and I run until we reach the point where the mine's corrugated fencing stops dead at a towering cliff. At that point our sole option is to turn left and follow the edge of the cliff and the winding creek bed below it. We run as fast as we are able, sloshing through the creek at times, toward the direction of town, apparently leaving the suited men well behind us. Cecil stops running when we get within sight of the town's buildings.

"What are you doing?" I ask.

"I'm going to sneak across the street to the inn and get all our stuff. We are going to have to hide somewhere for a little while—at least until everybody calms down—and then maybe we can try to work this all out."

"That doesn't make any sense," I say. "We didn't do anything wrong, and there is no reason for us to go into hiding. We just need to find the sheriff's office and straighten this out right now."

"We ain't got time to be arguing," Cecil gripes through gritted teeth. "We got all our stuff back there at the inn, and plus, I even hid half of my money in the mattress, and I ain't leaving that behind, They'll rifle through our stuff, and it'll all be gone. We can figure out what to do later, but for now we just need to get our stuff, especially my money."

He pauses for a moment, appearing to think, and says, "Here's how we're gonna do it."

Cecil yanks the handheld radio from his belt clip and points to some random spot through the woods near the edge of the road that runs alongside part of the town. "We're going to go over there, and we're going to turn our radios to, say, channel seven, so we'll be on our own channel. You can keep cover in the edge of the woods and watch out for me as I sneak over to our room. And you can let me know on the radio whether it's safe or not."

We get to about fifty feet from the edge of the road, when Cecil drops down, lies on his stomach, and motions for me to do the same. I drop down, and we slither on our bellies through a tangled obstacle of flesh-pricking briars until we stop on the edge of the road. Cecil instructs me to get my radio out, check the volume, and lie still. He reaches over, uproots a handful of saplings and several handfuls of tall weeds and grass, and covers my head and the upper half of my body with them.

"Okay, Greenway, I'm going for it. You keep a lookout and let me know if anybody's coming." He looks up and down the road to see if it's clear, jumps to his feet, and takes off across the street. My heart pounds with anxiety as he sprints across the massive grassy span that divides the road from the edge of the town. I relax when he takes cover behind a clump of pines a few buildings down from the inn. He calls me on the radio in a whisper. "Is it all clear? You see anybody?" I pause for a second to listen, paranoid that I can hear footsteps clicking through the creek bed that is more than a hundred yards behind me.

And after deciding that the sounds must be manufactured by my imagination, I scan the areas around Cecil and respond, "I can see a few people . . . looks like a woman and maybe a man, a few hundred feet to your left. Other than them, it's clear."

Cecil jumps up and sprints to the back side of the inn, kneeling between a row of shrubbery and a lattice trellis. "Still clear?" he asks.

"Yes. Please hurry," I say. The stress of it all is killing me. I listen behind me, thinking again that I hear rocks clicking as Cecil disappears around the corner of the inn. I lie still for the next few minutes, waiting to hear from him, hoping that he will reappear safely. Two or three minutes pass, and I hear nothing. I try calling him on the radio, "Cecil, where are you? Everything okay?" No reply. I try again. "Where are you?" Still no reply.

A pair of siren-blaring police cars comes speeding by. They get a little way past me, silence their sirens, and stop in the middle of the road. They pop their cars in reverse and start backing up, stopping almost in front of me. They must have seen me. I pick myself up to my hands and knees and get ready to run, but just when I get the feeling that they are about to make eye contact with me, they yank their steering wheels and speed off the side of the road, through the grassy area, stopping their cars behind the inn. I radio Cecil: "You'd better get out of there! Two carloads of cops just pulled in behind the inn."

Five men exit the two police cars with their guns drawn, as a dozen or more other armed men sprint through the alleyway and scatter around the back side of the inn. Cecil radios me: "I'm surrounded, Greenway. There is no way out. They're all over the place!"

18

I panic, fearing for my brother's life. Without much thought, I jump to my feet and yell as loudly as I can across the grassy span, in an attempt to distract the men who are after him. "Hey, you! I'm over here!" But none of the officers turn to acknowledge me, so I take off sprinting through the grassy area to get closer to them and shout again, "I'm over here!" But they still act like they can't hear me. All I know is, if I don't do something quick, they are going to end up killing him. Then the idea hits me, and it is likely the worst idea that I have ever had.

I pull my pistol from my holster, aim it toward the sky, and fire off three rounds. *Bang! Bang! Bang!* And before I can even re-holster my pistol, I see a stampede of maybe twenty men, with even more pouring through the alleyway, charging across the grassy span toward me.

I turn and take off running through the briar thicket. I find the creek bed and run a solid mile until the creek changes direction to flow beneath a stone-railed bridge to the opposite side of the road. I stop for a second to breathe and listen for the sound of the stampede approaching, but I can't hear anything other than the pounding of my heart.

"Where are you? Answer me," Cecil calls on the radio.

I peek up along the creek bed, making sure that no one is in sight before I respond. I whisper, "I don't know. I reckon I'm a mile down the creek from where we stopped. Where are you?"

"What in the world are you doing all the way down there? I'm up on the mountain—the one with the cliffs—beside the reservoir, and I have all our stuff. I was surrounded and thought I was going to die. Then I heard gunshots, and it's like everybody just vanished."

"Yeah, those were my gunshots. They vanished because they are chasing after me."

"What in the world, Greenway?!"

"Just stay there, and I'll find you. Be there as soon as I can. Just keep listening on your radio for me."

I run back to where the creek bends and look once again for the stampede, but there is no one in sight. I rip off my shirt and hang it on a low tree branch about fifty feet past the creek to make them think that I'm running in the other direction. I listen carefully one more time before I slip under the bridge to the other side of the road, and I run as fast as possible. I find the mountain where Cecil is and start climbing.

I get to the top of the mountain and follow the back side of the ridgeline toward the direction of town. Once I'm within sight of the town, I call Cecil on the radio. He gives me his exact location, and in a few minutes' time, we are back together again. As he walks over to meet me, I notice an odd expression on his face. He extends his arm, puts it around me, and hugs me for a second. "I don't know what you did back there, but you are crazy. You saved my life, brother."

"I don't know, either. I panicked when I seen that you got surrounded. I jumped out and started yelling at them. But I guess they didn't hear me, because it didn't work. Then I ran even closer and shouted at them, but that *still* didn't work. So I pulled out my pistol and fired it in the air, and, let me tell you, I had them all chasing after me. Every last one of them. Talk about scary."

"I'm impressed, brother. I didn't know you had it in you. That was some quick thinking, but you are lucky you didn't get yourself killed." He takes a minute to look me up and down and frowns. "Hey, where's your shirt?" he says.

"I hung it on a tree branch on the other side of the road to try to throw them off and make them think I went in the other direction."

"That was smart. It must have worked."

"Yeah, I guess so. I kept looking and listening for them the whole way up here, and there was no sign of them. They must have gone off chasing me in the other direction."

I sit down and try to catch my breath, and Cecil sits down beside me. "I just don't get it," I say. "I don't get how your gun going off got the whole town after us. How in the world did things get so out of control just over that?"

"I don't know," Cecil says. "And trust me, I'm sorry it happened. I know that I shouldn't have shot my gun. But you know as well as I do that I figured those bullets were fake—but never mind the gun for a second, I think that there has to be more to it than that. If you remember, they came speeding into the parking lot and sliding through the gravel and everything. They were acting all crazy before I ever even fired my pistol. They knew our names, and they were even demanding that we drop our pistols."

"You're right," I say. "There has to be more to it. You never pointed your gun at them or threatened them or anything, and they still tried to kill us. They must have shot at us a dozen times, and it is only by the grace of God that they didn't hit us."

"Well, they must think we did something," Cecil says. "And it must be pretty bad, whatever it is—bad enough for them to want to kill us over it."

"I don't know," I say. "All I can think is that I just want to crawl under a rock and die."

I start to cry as soon as the words leave my mouth, but then the thought hits me that there is no use in crying. Crying won't do me a bit of good. "Everything was so perfect a couple of days ago," I say. "In fact, they were better than they had ever been. But now look at us. Things are worse than they've ever been. How can that be? I guess Dad and Uncle Tibbs were right about us. And maybe we should have listened to them, but here we are now—ruined, just ruined. And worse than before."

I can't help but cry again. It still won't do me a bit of good, but this time I can't help it. I have to cry; there is just no stopping it. All I can think is, *Why does life have to be so hard?* And how could I not cry over a thought like that? I feel so hopeless about it all, and there is nothing I can do to change it. Nothing I can do but pray. I'm not sure how God is going to get us out of this one, but I'm going to pray, anyway.

Cecil places his hand on my shoulder, and I assume it's an attempt to comfort me. But after he pats and squeezes my shoulder a few times, he pushes me over. I sit back up at once, and then he slaps me on the back of the head. "Come on, brother," he says, "quit your whining; we're going to get through this. This isn't the first time we've had trouble, and it sure won't be the last. If you think about it, our whole life has been nothing but trouble, but we always seem to get through it, somehow."

"Yeah, but this time it's different," I suggest. "It looks like everybody wants us dead this time."

Cecil and I decide to hide out here for now. We figure it must be the safest place around because, from here, we have a full view of town and can easily escape down the back of the mountain if anyone sees us. For the rest of the day, we hide and watch while dozens of uniformed police officers, with their arms outstretched, holding their pistols and rifles in firing position, scour the streets and alleyways and the woods that surround the town. We observe them as they peek maliciously around every corner, inside every structure, and behind every shrub. It seems unrealistic to think that this is all caused by my brother and me.

That night, we agree to sleep in shifts so we can continue to keep an eye on things. Cecil sleeps for a few hours while I keep a lookout, and then Cecil keeps watch while I sleep. Flashlights and voices scurry through the darkness of the night and remain until the light of day.

The following morning, the search appears to cease. But around noon it starts back up again but with twice as many men as yesterday. We watch news trucks dribble in every so often, while others set up large tents and smaller canopies in the grassy area.

As the hours of the day drip away, those familiar thirst and hunger pains return to my flesh, and I find myself talking less about all the activity that is going on in the town below and more about the things I would like to eat. Cecil seems annoyed by this, but when I'm hungry, I find it impossible not to talk about food. I am craving Mom and Auntie Rose's cooking so much right now that I can't stand it. We might have been poor back home in Colby Valley, but we were never hungry.

Shortly after sunset, Cecil catches me off guard, by calling dibs, and instructs me to keep the first watch. I was hoping that

I could sleep first this time because the one thing about sleeping is you can easily forget about how hungry you are.

As Cecil sleeps, I sit here fighting my drowsiness and hunger pains. After about two hours of his annoying snores, I give him a nudge. "Wake up. It's my turn," I say. But he doesn't budge, so this time I shake him.

"I heard you, and if you keep shaking me, I'm going to punch you."

"Well, get up, then. It's my turn to get some sleep," I say.

"But I just fell asleep; it ain't your turn yet."

"No, you didn't. You've been asleep for two hours."

But no sooner do I spit out those last words than his selfish snores rekindle. I love my brother, but he makes me so mad sometimes. As I sit here, watching him sleep so comfortably, my mind begins to wander. Before I know it, I consider the idea of sneaking into town to find something to eat. I know it's a terrible idea, and I am trying to resist it, but this drowsiness, coupled with my grumbling stomach, has me feeling a little bit reckless.

I creep down the steep mountain, hoping that neither Cecil nor the townspeople will hear me. And after a few minutes, I find myself standing at the edge of the reservoir considering my next move. I don't see any movement anywhere in town and begin to feel safe. I scoot along the edge of the reservoir until I reach the upper section of town. The glow from the streetlights is intense, so I seek the less revealing shadows of the town's buildings. While I linger safely in the shadows, I see a group of wood-sided buildings that look promising: Catsed Food Market, Wringley's Produce, and May's Sweets.

Crawling on all fours like a dog, I sneak around to the back of the cluster of buildings, hoping to find something within the dumpsters that's expired but still edible. I check the one behind Catsed first, only to find empty boxes. I scour one more trash bin that I assume is shared by Wringley's and May's Sweets, and I get lucky—well, not fried chicken lucky, but as lucky as one could get under the current circumstances. Underneath a bundle of rotten carrots, which I can't stand the taste of, I find a whole box of mushy onions, a tray of expired cellophane-wrapped chocolate drops, and a bag of oblong, multicolored sweets—perhaps jelly beans. But whatever they are, I manage to eat a handful of them before filling my pockets with the rest to save for later. I then load my stomach full of chocolate drops and raw onions. It's about the worst combination of flavors imaginable, but they satisfy my hunger pains.

With the protective cover of shadows, I sneak around the cluster of buildings to make my way back to the mountain. But as I turn the corner, I gasp. It's Cecil. No, it's not him standing there in the flesh—it's worse than that. It's a black-and-white poster taped to a lamppost with his picture on it next to mine. In large print, the poster reads:

WANTED

CECIL AND GREENWAY POCHAW
$1,000,000 REWARD

This has to be a joke. How is it that we have a million-dollar bounty on our heads? It terrifies me to think of all the possible reasons for such a large bounty. We must be in more trouble than I thought.

I rip the poster from the lamppost, fold it up, and slip it into my sock. As I turn around to head back toward the hill, I panic. Two men have stopped in front of me. One of them holds up another copy of the wanted poster identical to the one I just tore down. I can tell immediately he is comparing my face to the image on the paper. "It's him," one of the men barks before reaching out to grab me. But I'm still not wearing a shirt, and he is unable to find purchase on my bare skin. There is nothing for him to grab on to. His hand slides across my sweaty shoulder as I duck down, make my escape dashing between the two of them, and slip away in the darkness.

After several minutes of running through the darkness, I return to my hideaway on the hill. I sit on the ground and allow my heart to slow before I attempt to wake Cecil. When I figure my heart rate has slowed enough and I've stopped sweating, I give him a nudge to wake him. After I explain that he has already slept most of the night, he agrees to give me my turn.

I fall deep asleep in the span of a couple of seconds and dream plenty, but it doesn't seem to last for long. I'm awakened by a sharp slap against the back of my leg. I force my tired eyes open, notice the rising sun, and try to drift off to sleep again. But he slaps me even more sharply. "Get up," he demands softly and yet forcefully through gritted teeth.

"Not yet. Leave me alone, and let me have just a few more minutes."

He motions for me to be quiet with his pointer finger pressed against his lips, and then stretches out his other arm and points to an area below us. I look down, and the slumber in my eyes dissolves. About thirty rifle-toting men and several dogs are stepping in our direction. Without another word of discussion, Cecil and I crawl until we reach the back side of the mountain. As soon as we get to our feet and manage to take our first few steps toward escaping, we hear the dogs behind us start yipping and howling. We take off running.

We run until I can no longer stand, but we're well past the point where the dogs' barking can no longer be heard. "Let's stop here," I say, looking down at my watch. "I can't go any farther. We've been running for over an hour. I think we're far enough away."

19

We drop down and prop our backs against a pair of trees growing several feet apart. I look over at Cecil and watch as he digs into his front pants pocket. He pulls out the pouch of cigarette tobacco and cigarette papers he bought back in Colby Valley. He unseals the small pouch and sniffs inside. I just look away, trying to hide my smile. I can't believe that he is even thinking about having a cigarette after all the running we just did. He's still out of breath, and he's not even a smoker. I don't know what he's trying to prove, but I watch as he pulls a single paper from the pack, folds it in half, and drops a few slivers of tobacco into the fold. He then shuffles the lot between his thumbs and fingers, licks one side of the paper, and then rolls it into a dog-turd-shaped cigarette. He wedges the crumbled mess between his two dusty and cracked lips, sets a match to it, and lights it. He inhales the thick white smoke and chokes. "Ya want one?" he asks. I deal him a don't-be-stupid look and refuse the offer.

As Cecil puffs on his cigarette, I just sit and relax, looking out through the trees. I try to rehearse in my mind how I'm going to tell Cecil that I snuck into town and found the wanted poster, but I guess I'll be much better off if I don't mention it. He'd never let me hear the end of it, especially after all the running that we just did. Maybe I'll find a better opportunity to show him later. But I'd say the best thing for me to do now is just to keep quiet and relax while I can.

My drowsiness returns, and through heavy eyes, I look over at Cecil as he finishes off his cigarette. He takes one last puff, exhales the thick smoke through his nostrils, and kicks away a pile of leaves. He takes the filthy remains of his cigarette and pushes it into the bare spot he just made. Twisting the heel of his shoe, he grinds the cigarette the rest of the way into the ground.

Just as I start to nod off, Cecil speaks. "Something smells awful funny," he says. He leans over and sniffs my head. "That's the rotten smell that I've been catching wind of all morning."

I push him away. "What's your problem?" I ask. "The only thing I smell is your nasty cigarette."

"You smell like a nasty old onion or something. What in the crap have you been into? Ain't no wonder why those dogs were howling at us."

"Why don't you just leave me alone so I can get some sleep? In case you don't remember, you're the one that got to sleep almost all night."

Cecil scoots back next to his tree, while appearing to be deep in thought. But I don't care what he thinks; I'm going back to sleep.

I wake up a while later, feeling more rested, but my forehead is sweating plenty. It's about midday, when the sun is at its fullest and steadily heating up the sky. I look over to where Cecil had been sitting, and he is gone.

Just when I'm about to start worrying, he steps out from behind a thick patch of pine trees. His bright eyes and slight grin tell me he's pleased and a little excited about something. "Come on," he says. "You're not going to believe this. Grab our sacks and follow me. But put on a shirt or these pine trees are going to tear you to pieces." He disappears back into the pine thicket, and I jump to my feet, put on a shirt, grab our feed sacks, and follow him along a path through the pines.

The scent of pine fills my nose as I swim through the green river of sappy needles, trying to keep up with Cecil. I follow him for a few more minutes, until we come out into an opening, and I can't believe my eyes. It's water—a big pond. "Thank God," Cecil says. "I thought I was going to die of thirst."

He kneels down, scoops up some water in the palm of his hand, and starts to drink. "Whoa, wait a minute," I say. "I don't think that is near safe enough to drink; it's awful murky."

"I already had some and couldn't care less—I'm thirsty."

"You're going to end up getting deathly ill if you keep it up. Trust me. We had better at least boil it and sterilize it before you drink any more. All sorts of parasites live in pond water, and I once read that a man can die of the poops for drinking it as it stands."

"Okay, we'll boil 'er, then. I sure don't want to go down in history as the guy who pooped himself to death."

I pull the tin kettle from my sack and dip it in the filthy pond water as Cecil arranges a mound of twigs on the bank and sets a match to it. I set the kettle on the pile of flaming twigs and wait for the water to boil. We watch as it bubbles and steams for a few minutes, until we both agree that it has boiled enough. Cecil yanks the kettle from the fire and dips it a few inches deep into the pond water to help it cool. After a few more minutes of watching the steam dissipate, Cecil and I pass the kettle back and forth until we're both full of the lukewarm, particle-rich fluid.

After putting on another kettle of water to boil for later, Cecil and I scour the pond in search of food. It doesn't take us but a minute or two to realize that there is enough food around here to last us—and maybe a few hundred more people—for a lifetime. There is stuff crawling, swimming, and hopping everywhere.

Cecil flips a small chunk of wood into the pond, and dozens of starving bluegills slice through the water to peck at it. Shortly after the bluegills churn the water, curious turtles appear and swim to the edge of the pond. I hold out a white splinter of wood, and a few of the turtles climb the grassy bank and charge my hand to try it. One of the turtles, with wide eyes and almost bronze pupils, stretches its elastic neck and nips at the splinter. He withdraws his head slowly and waits, as if I might consider swapping the splinter for something edible.

My heart begins to fill with sympathy for the bubbly-eyed creature because he looks hungry, so I look around, hoping to find something within reach that may satisfy its stomach. I turn and scan the grassy bank, without the slightest clue of what a turtle might eat. I turn over a rock and find a sow bug and figure I'll try to give it to him. I stretch my arm out to grab it, but before I can even pinch it between my fingers, I hear a hollow thump and get this feeling of warm liquid running down the back of my neck. I turn around and see Cecil smiling proudly while holding a log the size and shape of a baseball bat.

"He didn't even bat an eye. I knocked him cold," Cecil boasts. I look down and see the poor, once bubbly-eyed turtle. His shell is split from end to end, and his legs are twitching. And before I can say anything, Cecil rears back the club and whops him again. "He's big enough to feed the both of us, and then some," he adds.

With my stomach still full and somewhat upset from the onions and chocolate I consumed last night, it's easy for me to be saddened by the crushed state of my newfound friend. But I guess it's more important that my brother gets to eat. I watch as

Cecil flips open his pocketknife, makes a few careful incisions around the shell, and peels the turtle like a coconut. He guts it and then pierces a twig through the butchered meat and holds it over the fire. The flames dance and kiss the chunks of meat, creating a delicious smell and making it easy for me to forget about the poor turtle.

During the next few days, Cecil and I more or less make this place our home. By now, we've already entered into a friendship with most of the creatures that live here—well, at least the ones we haven't tried to turn into breakfast or supper. I can't say I've had much luck befriending them grouchy geese, though, and I haven't even tried to eat one of them yet. All you have to do is walk past one, and they all start hissing at you. That's all they ever do, and they are pretty much worthless, as far as I can see.

It has been an interesting few days, but during all our time relaxing here, I haven't been able to get Cecil to have a conversation about what we're going to do next. He acts like he would like to stay here forever, but I can't shake the feeling that if we hang around here too long, somebody will find us, and they will be cracking their pistols at us the moment they do. I don't want to leave this place no more than he does because there is plenty of food and water here, but I think that it's time we move on. I have to try and convince him somehow.

"I know you don't want to talk about it," I say. "But I think that we need to. I feel like we need to move on and go somewhere else. I don't think it's safe that we hang around here much longer. I got a terrible feeling about it."

He looks over at me and scowls. "I told ya we'd talk about it later," he says.

But I persist. "Well, when do you think you'll feel like talking about it? We need to have this discussion."

"We don't need to do anything, and you are starting to get on my nerves. I don't want to deal with you. Just go on and leave me alone."

"But Cecil, don't you think we should be doing something? I know it's nice here and all, but don't you think we're pushing our luck? We aren't that far from town, and somebody is bound to stumble upon us and start shooting."

And for the first time since we left Colby Valley, Cecil raises his voice at me. "I told you to go on and leave me alone! Just go on."

I can see that I've done nothing but waste my time trying to have this conversation. I suppose I could have gained more by trying to talk to one of them lousy geese. I grab my feed sack and take off walking.

"Where are you going?" Cecil asks.

"You must have a short memory because you just told me to go on. And I figure that I can use some time by myself, anyway, so I'm going to the other side of the pond to set up camp somewhere else. You just let me know when you're ready to move on. And leave me alone until then."

Deep down I am hoping that my threat to camp elsewhere is enough to pressure him to move on, but based on the look on his face, I think he's relieved at my potential absence. "Carry your whiny butt on, then," he says. "That suits me just fine! I'm tired of looking at you, anyway."

Honestly, I am feeling the same way. There is only so much time you can spend around a person before you need a break. I sling my feed bag over my shoulder and hike to the other side of the pond. Then I search for a comfortable place to camp. I notice a fair-looking and out-of-the-way spot near a small stream trickling from the pond. I make my way to it, pushing through a thicket of mountain laurels, then drop down and prop myself up against a small bundle of trees. I wind up spending the rest of the day in the same spot, just hearing my own breathing.

The following morning, I wake up alone and well rested, appreciating the break from Cecil. I sit in silence for a moment, allowing my brain to also wake up. Through the thicket in front of me, I can hear faint sounds of the forest floor being trampled. Perhaps a creature that will be suitable for breakfast is heading my way. I hush my breathing and listen carefully. A few loud thumps bounce from the forest floor, and I start thinking that whatever it is just might be a little too big for breakfast.

Feeling worried, I sneak backward and slide in among the mountain laurels to hide. The thumping grows louder and becomes more frequent, as whatever it is apparently gets closer. After a few more minutes, I hear what sounds like the heel-to-toe steps of a human foot. I figure it's Cecil looking for me; I suppose he misses me already.

I peek out from behind the laurels and wait for him to appear, but then the noise stops. I pay close attention and imagine I hear several whispers and maybe even the sound of a man clearing his throat. The thumps appear again, and the patch of laurels in front of me begins to fill with shakes and cracks. Perhaps I'm still half asleep and not thinking too clearly just yet, but it sounds like several people are heading toward me. A rush of adrenaline fills me, and I pull the pistol from my pants and anticipate my escape.

20

My heart starts thumping against my chest, rattling my shirt pocket. Sweat pools and drips from my brow despite the fact that it is a cool, comfortable morning. I turn and visualize a path through the laurel thicket. I slowly place one foot in front of the other and prepare to run. But before I can even swing another step, a deep and somewhat annoyed voice grabs my attention. "Get on the ground," it demands. "Take another step, and you're finished."

I stand still with my back toward the man, my leg still stretching and ready to run. I immediately hear the sound of a few more people approaching. And in the distance, I hear what sounds like a coon dog let out a big howl. Then a different man speaks. "Oh, just shoot him." Another man shouts, "You better watch him! He's sneaky."

They let off me for a second, and some of them start whispering among themselves. Then, all of a sudden, I hear a familiar voice—it's my brother's. My heart sinks at the sound of it. "Greenway, they got us. There is no way out—turn yourself in."

"You hear that, boy?" another man says. "You had better listen to your brother."

The rest of the people take turns shouting at me and threatening me with every kind of possible punishment if I don't turn around. But I stand in silence, my back still toward them and my adrenaline-filled feet still ready to run. I don't know what to do, but I sure don't want to turn around.

The sound of a shotgun being pumped echoes behind me, and one of the men demands that I turn and face him. And for some reason, all the threats and shouting coming from this tag team angers me to my core. Without even thinking about what I am doing, I spin and point my pistol at the first head I see. The man drops his rifle, and his legs go limp as his hands go up. The other men have guns pointed at me, but I keep my gun held steadily at the man.

These men are not uniformed police officers; they're ordinary men wearing flannels and bib overalls. I assume they all are just bounty hunters merely trying to cash in on a million-dollar reward. I search for Cecil's face as my eyes scan through the crowd, but I don't see him anywhere. "Where is my brother?" I ask.

"Drop that gun, you stupid boy. Can't you see you're out-gunned?" the man closest to me demands. His legs are shaking like jelly, but his hands remain in the air while he stares down the barrel of my pistol.

For some reason, the "stupid boy" insult magnifies my anger, and my voice elevates to a tone that I never knew it had. "I got three bullets," I shout, "and from where I'm standing, I can take out two or three of you before you even know what hit you. Now, where is my brother? Tell me!" I demand, hoping they don't call my bluff. Yes, I am angry, but I would never willingly hurt anybody.

A few of the men near the back of the crowd start laughing. They separate as two of them produce Cecil. They grab him by the shoulders and yank him from the ground, forcing him to stand. Half of his head and face is soaked with blood. "What'd they do to you, Cecil? Are you okay?" I ask.

Cecil stares at me open-mouthed, as if he is shocked at my behavior. He doesn't respond to my question.

"Tell him," demands one of the men standing next to him.

"I don't know what happened," Cecil cries. "Something smashed me in the head, and when I woke up, two men were dragging me, and my head was busting—"

"He doesn't know 'cause he was sleeping," the man says. "But if it's that important to you, the butt of my rifle happened to meet his head a time or two when he was sucking his thumb."

"You idiot," I shout. "He's losing a lot of blood. Somebody needs to help him."

Cecil speaks in a weakened tone, "Greenway, please, just turn yourself in. We're outnumbered."

"Listen to your brother," the man with my gun pointed at his head says. "You're already looking at life in prison, and if you pull that trigger, your life will be ending right where you stand. It's your choice."

"Life in prison for what?" I ask.

"Are you really that stupid, boy? They haven't found the bodies yet, but there is enough evidence to put you and your brother away forever. For murder."

"You're out of your mind; we've never murdered anybody" I say.

"But you two sure murdered those girls."

My anger has increased to a level that is causing me to shake. "What are you talking about? We did no such thing!" I manage to shout.

"Do the names Cass and Janie mean anything to you? Or did you even know their names?"

"You're crazy; we just met them girls."

"Yeah, you met 'em, and then you took their lives."

A shirtless man wearing faded blue bib overalls makes his way to the front of the crowd. "That's about enough of this crap," he says. "Just put the pistol down, and we will sort this all out at the sheriff's office."

I disobey the man and leave my gun drawn, while I try to decide what to do.

Though I don't understand how this has happened, it seems that my only options involve death or life in prison. But then again, maybe if they take me to the sheriff, I can tell him everything that happened and work it all out. But at the same time, I don't have any reason to believe that these savages will even get me there alive. They seem like the type that would just kill you for fun. Cecil speaks up again, interrupting my thoughts. "Daggone it. Don't be getting yourself killed. There ain't much you can do but put down your gun and hand yourself over."

I grow weary of weighing my options and decide that I'm not about to take either one of them. I think I'll be much better off if I just run, and I am just too mad to simply give up. And so, without another second's thought, I lift my head and look out through the trees behind the men. I deal them a short laugh and say, "Well, Cecil. It looks as though we're no longer outnumbered, as you say. It appears that our own reinforcements finally decided to show up." All the men, including Cecil, turn their heads to see what I am talking about. As soon as their attention leaves me, I rise to my tiptoes, turn around, and, with long strides, disappear into the dense mountain laurels.

Within seconds, the men realize that I have tricked them and start firing their guns madly in my direction. All around me, I can hear speeding bullets tearing through the laurel leaves and branches. I try running faster, but every step I take seems to be in slow motion. I search for a large tree or a high rise in the elevation to hide behind, but I can't find anything that might protect me. All I can do is run and hope that every new step I take will be quicker than the last.

Suddenly, the shooting stops and the threat of the dogs takes over. They are stirring up an awful fuss: barking, yipping, and growling, all in the same breath. Even though I'm still in danger, I feel relieved. I would choose a ball of fur over a ball of lead coming at me any day. I rip my sweaty shirt off and sling it high in a tree, hoping that it will be enough to satisfy the dogs, and I run like a maniac.

After a few minutes, the mountain laurels begin to thin out, making it easier for me to get through. I stop in a small clearing and listen as well as my ringing ears will allow me to. I can hear the dogs a little ways back, howling like they've treed a coon, so I take it that my idea of throwing my shirt in the tree worked. I don't know how long it will keep them busy, but I sure as heck won't be staying around to find out. I continue in the same direction as before, and in a few minutes, I find myself poking into the sky, standing on the edge of a dreadful cliff.

The cliff extends to my left and right, as far as I can see, so I have no choice but to find a way down. Small saplings hide the exact edge of the cliff, and there is no way of telling where the ground ends. I put my pistol back in my pants, lie on my stomach, and sliver through the saplings to investigate. I reach the edge and immediately realize I'm facing a terribly deep drop, but thick clumps of grass on the edge obscure my view of the face of the cliff, and I have no way of telling if there is a way to climb down.

I start tearing away at the grass with my bare hands, yanking it from the loose soil, roots and all. Big clods of dirt separate from the edge and plunge hundreds of feet into a pool of green water at the bottom of the cliff. With my obstructions now uprooted, I peer over the edge to find out what the face of the cliff looks like. And I'm struck with terror. I can see that the face of the cliff is several feet behind me, and what I'm lying on is merely an unstable lip of root-enforced soil.

21

I consider facing my fear of heights and jumping into the pool of green water, but from where I am, the pool appears to be as small as it is shallow. So, if I jump, I risk landing in only a few feet of water; or I could even miss the water altogether. As I crawl backward to the comfort of solid ground, a casket-sized chunk of dirt breaks loose and plunges from the edge. I try crawling faster, when another chunk drops, then another. The soil beneath me begins to puff and pop, as quarter-sized pores open up, allowing the loose soil on top to fill the voids below. A deep crack, appearing at the edge of the cliff, opens up, branches out, and races past me So I jump to my feet and run.

I make it safely to the edge of the woods, where the soil is no longer separating, only to find that awful bunch of trigger-happy men standing about twenty feet in front of me. They are standing as links in a length of straightened chain, focusing their eyes in a trance-like stare down the barrels of their loaded rifles, shotguns, and pistols. "I'd say you're pretty darn lucky you didn't get sucked right off the cliff," one of the men says. He empties his cheek of chewing tobacco fluid with a casual spit. "You know there ain't any way of running now."

Ignoring the fact that I have at least two dozen guns pointing at me, I reach for my pistol. I have the handle gripped in my hand, but before I can even raise it, the men threaten me collectively with death if I budge it another inch. "Okay, I will drop it," I say.

I scan the crowd, seeking a bit of encouragement from Cecil, but I don't see him. So I decide I won't drop the pistol yet. "Where is my brother?"

"Don't worry," the tobacco-spitting man says. "He is taken care of. He was bleeding right much, so they went on and hauled him to the hospital. Now, drop that pistol and turn yourself in before you wind up getting killed."

The tobacco-spitting man instructs the others to stay put and keep a good eye on me. He inches over to me, not the least intimidated by the loaded pistol in my hand. He gets about ten feet in front of me and stops. "Okay," he says calmly. "I'm going to toss you these handcuffs. Now drop that pistol, so you can catch 'em." The man winks secretly at me and deals me an open-eyed squint.

I study the language of his eyes but can't even begin to understand the motive of his wink. He takes another step toward me and whispers through his teeth, "I'm here to help you; now, do what I say." He winks again and yells, "Now, listen to me. Drop the gun! Right now! Do it now!" He deals me another wink and another open-eyed squint, so I do exactly as he says and drop the pistol.

The old man dips his fingers into his shirt pocket, pulls out a pair of handcuffs and slings them at me. They fly past my head and spill to the ground, and the man chirps with anger. "This is not the time for games. What's wrong with you?" He winks again, grunts forcefully, wipes a stream of sweat from his forehead with the sleeve of his flannel, and says, "I think you're trying to take me for a fool; you didn't even try to catch the handcuffs."

"Sorry," I say. "What do you want me to do?"

"Don't you budge an inch. I'll fetch them."

The old man returns his attention to the clan of gunslingers and says, "This man's a bag full o' tricks; you all watch him close while I get the cuffs." A few of the men nod their heads in agreement and cock the levers of their rifles for show. The old man hurries toward me, kicks the pistol away from me, and walks past me. Naturally, my eyes follow him. I watch as he picks up the handcuffs, takes a few steps, and peeks over the edge of the crumbling cliff. He returns with the handcuffs dangling from his pinky finger. He positions himself in front of me, with his back to all the men, and he licks the inside of his lower lip and spits on the ground.

"Okay, now. No more games. Let's get this over with and put these handcuffs on." He blinks rapidly a few times and says, "Now, don't try to fight it, man. Just poke your wrist out here, nice and easy, while I slide these cuffs on you." He winks again and deals me a another open-eyed squint. I think he is signaling me to disobey, so I play along and pull my hands away from him.

The old man takes another step toward me, softens his eyes, and grins secretly. He broadens his shoulders, throws me another wink, and continues, but this time he is yelling. "Give me your hands now before I take 'em from you!" He bites the cuffs with his teeth to free his hands, reaches out, and grabs both of my arms. My arms dangle in the man's hands, but he acts as though I'm resisting and that he can't extend my arms. "I warned you, man!" he shouts.

He then throws himself at me, knocks me to the ground, digs his knees into my stomach, pins my shoulders to the ground with stiff arms, and whispers through his teeth, "Wrestle me now. Hurry." He releases the pressure from my shoulders and shoots me a serious look, so I start wiggling my shoulders and rocking my upper body from side to side. The gunslingers in the background roar with laughter and cheer on the old man.

I'm feeling uncertain about what I should do, but I reach out with both hands, grab ahold of his shirt, and start pulling at it. He then pulls his hands from my shoulder, grabs me under my arms, latches to me, and forces me into a roll down the small incline. We bounce over jagged rocks and plow over small saplings, and before I can even consider all the possible benefits of our charade, I find myself sailing off the edge of the cliff. And a few seconds later, my flesh smacks the green pool of water.

I sink like a stone to the bottom of the green pool and thrust myself back up to the oxygen-rich sky. I search for the face of the crazy old man, not sure if I should greet him with anger or gratitude for the stunt he just pulled. "Are you nuts?" I ask. He ignores my question and swims for the bank, so I follow. After struggling to pull myself from the water, I turn to face the old man and find myself struck with confusion. This doesn't look like the same old man that I just fell through the sky with.

The man who rolled me off the cliff had a headful of patchy gray hair, but this man's head is draped with shoulder-length black hair. "What happened to your gray hair?" I ask.

"That was just a wig. It came off when I hit the water." He smiles, wrings the water out of his hair with his hands, and sits down on the bank. "You really don't recognize who I am, do you?"

"No, I don't, but you strike me as somebody who needs to have his head examined," I say sarcastically. I laugh, but I'm being serious at the same time. "I can't believe you just rolled us off that cliff!"

The man chuckles and peels a phony frosted goatee from his face. "Do you recognize me now?"

And to my surprise, I see a man sitting before me that everyone back home calls Stinky Joe, a man I've talked to only a few times and know very little about. All I can tell you about him is that he lives in Colby Valley, and a lot of the townsfolk are mean to him because he lives in an old shack by the trash dump.

"I can't believe it," I say. "It's Stinky Joe from Colby Valley! But now that I'm hearing myself say it, I get the feeling that's not your name, is it?"

He smiles with his slim lips, revealing his front teeth, and says, "Well, no, it's not. But I don't mind you calling me that. That's what almost everyone else calls me; but if you want to know, my real name is Samuel."

"Sorry, I never knew that. I'm sorry I called you that, but I'll call you by your real name from now on. I don't mean any disrespect."

"Don't worry about it. Trust me, it doesn't bother me," he says.

I look down and notice the skin on my chest is turning dark red from slapping the water so hard, and it is starting to burn. But it seems pointless to whine about it, so I attempt to ignore the pain and say, "Well, how in the world did you end up here in Griggs Town? Did you come down here for work?"

"No. I came here just to fetch you and Cecil. It's all over the place back home that you two are wanted for murder, and everybody who knows you both knows there ain't no way it's true. So, your mama and Rose came down to my place, knocked on my door, and they were just a-crying and a-begging that I come and fetch you two and bring you back home so they could help you sort it all out. I told 'em I'd be happy to do it but couldn't afford it 'cause work is slow. And wouldn't you know, they pulled out an envelope and handed me a twenty-dollar bill and even baked me a cake for the road—I ate 'most the whole thing on the ride here."

"I don't know what to say," I respond. "I just don't. I can't believe that you came all the way down here just for us, and I can't believe that you risked your life to rescue me. Nobody has ever done anything like that for me. Nobody. I'm sorry that I said you need to have your head examined earlier. I feel ashamed about it, and I don't mean it. I was just in shock that you rolled me off that cliff."

"Well, I was happy to do it, and don't worry about it," he says. He then sticks his finger into his mouth, uses it to hook to the wad of chewing tobacco that he has been holding in his jaw, and slings it through the trees like a baseball. He wipes his tobacco-stained finger on his wet pants and says, "But we better get moving so we can bust your brother out of the hospital and get you both back to Colby Valley." He stands up and starts walking away. "Follow me," he says.

Samuel leads me quickly through the woods, and in a few minutes, we find ourselves standing within sight of the sheriff's office. He points to a light-blue pickup truck with rusted out fenders sitting in the parking lot. "That's my truck," he says. "You wait right here while I get it."

I watch nervously from the edge of the woods as he sloshes through the parking lot in his wet shoes, leaving a small puddle of water behind him with each step. The door hinge on his truck pops and screeches as he opens the door. Once he is seated, he slams the door, cranks the exhaustless engine, and squeals the tires as he speeds through the parking lot. He slows the truck at the edge of the parking lot to crawl across a short ditch. After he manages to clear it, he slaps the gas pedal again and darts through the woods beside me, plowing over dozens of small pine trees. I scan the sidewalk in front of the sheriff's office astonished that he managed to not draw any attention from anyone. As soon as I hear the engine stop, I look for a path around the bent trees to find him.

Samuel exits the truck, smiles, and says, "Did you see anybody?"

I look on in amazement. "No, not a one," I say. "I don't know how in the world you managed to do what you just did right in front of the sheriff's office without anybody seeing you, but you did it!"

"Well, that's because nobody is there. Everybody's out somewhere looking for you," he says. Samuel hurries around and drops the tailgate on his truck, revealing an empty bed. "What do you see now?" he asks.

"I don't see anything."

"That's good, because you weren't supposed to."

He grabs the open tailgate and pushes in on it and a large piece of steel that is covering the length of the bed springs up, exposing a hidden compartment. "This hidden place under the bed is how I plan to get you and Cecil out of here without anybody seeing you," he says.

"What? Am I supposed to be getting in there right now?"

"No. Not now. We got to fetch Cecil first." He grabs a large olive-drab duffel bag from the compartment, empties its contents on the ground, and continues, "And we are going to need this to do it."

22

"What is all that?" I ask.

"I found all this over the years at the trash dump. These will be our disguises. We'll have to use them to sneak your brother out of the hospital. You're going to like this," he says. He chuckles as he sorts through the pile, occasionally tossing an item for me to catch. "Change into these clothes," he says. "And use this razor and the side-view mirror on my truck to shave the stubble off your face. We got to make you look younger."

He tosses me the razor and a can of shaving cream and then disappears behind the truck to change his clothes. I hurry to shave my face in front of the mirror, and then I dig through the handful of landfill-scented clothes he gave me, only to find that my disguise will somehow be a pair of blaze orange shorts and a red T-shirt with a cartoon eagle across the front. The shirt doesn't look too bad, but the shorts don't have any pockets, so I guess I will have to hide my money somewhere in Samuel's truck.

"Hey, Samuel."

"Yes?" he answers from behind the truck.

"If you don't mind me asking, what is it exactly that I'm supposed to be? What look am I going for here?"

He laughs, and says, "Don't you worry; there is more to it than that. Just put it on, and I'll show you the rest as soon as I finish getting dressed."

I remove my wet shoes and my wet pants. And to my surprise, the jelly beans, or whatever they were, that I had obtained from the dumpster behind May's Sweets a few nights ago, had managed to dissolve themselves in my wet pants pocket and stain the skin on my right leg a mixture of green, orange, and purple. I don't know if Samuel will approve of my new leg color or not, but I go ahead and slip on the clothes that he gave me. The shorts are about two sizes too small, and the red eagle T-shirt is too short—so short that my belly button keeps peeping out.

I am a bit jealous of Samuel as he appears from around the corner of his truck wearing a nicer outfit than mine: dark blue jeans; a checkered green-and-white, button-up, short-sleeved flannel shirt; dark-blue suspenders; and a pair of light-tan work boots. "What do you think about my new look?" he asks.

"Oh, it suits you, I suppose. But what do you think about mine? I feel like I look like an idiot. And look at my leg—I had wet candy in my pocket when we went in the water, and then *this* happened."

Samuel fights to hide his laughter before answering. "I must admit, it does look ridiculous," he says, "but I think you can pull it off."

"What is it that I'm trying to pull off here?"

"The idea is that I'm going to take you to the hospital emergency room and act like you're hurt or sick, but we got to make sure that no one can recognize us. Once we're in, I'm going to create a distraction so that we can sneak Cecil out of there."

He rushes over to me, peels the lid from a cookie tin, and hands it to me. "Here is a wig and some different teeth. Put these over your real teeth and bite down hard to lock them into place. The wig is self-explanatory, but when you put it on, be sure you get all your hair tucked under it." Before I can even finish squeezing my head into this ridiculous, short and fire-engine-red wig and cramming these oversized plastic teeth into my mouth, Samuel has already embellished himself with short white hair, white eyebrows, and a full white beard.

I hurry to finish tucking my hair under my wig, while watching curiously as he smears light-colored makeup all over his face and finishes off his look with what he calls "age spots" that he attempts to mimic with a light-brown marker. He inspects my wig. After he plucks at it and teases it to his satisfaction, he grabs a ring of odd-looking keys from his truck, slips them into his pocket, and signals me to go. And with Samuel looking like a freckled albino mountain man, and me looking like, well, an idiot, we exit the woods in search of the hospital. I am afraid these disguises will look so ridiculous that there will be no way for this to work, and the thought of him needing to have his head examined returns to me once again.

With little to no trouble, we find the hospital emergency room entrance. After Samuel instructs me to clutch my right side and not speak a word, we enter the building in a rush. My gut fills with jitters as I enter the lobby and see a uniformed officer chatting with a few of the gunslingers who had me cornered earlier. And as soon as they make eye contact with me, my heart begins beating against my chest. I just hope they don't recognize me.

"We got an emergency, mister," Samuel manages to say in a convincing elderly voice.

The men look at us with dubious eyes. "What's wrong with the boy?" the officer asks, lowering his eyes and appearing to stare at my candy-stained leg. "Is his leg hurt?"

"His leg just started doing that," Samuel says. "But his side is hurting something awful, like he's got a ruptured appendix."

The uniformed man ejects from his chair. "Come right this way," he says.

He leads us past the registration window and through a set of double doors, then stops us at the nurses' station and declares our emergency to a group of nurses. Two of the nurses rush around from behind the counter and seat me in a wheelchair. With one of the ladies pushing, the other one escorting, and the freckled albino mountain man limping behind, they zip me down a narrow hallway and wheel me into a room, two doors past a room that is being guarded by two deputies. A room that is undoubtedly holding my brother, Cecil.

The ladies help me into a back-lying position on the bed, record my blood pressure and temperature, promise me a doctor soon, and hurry away. Old Man Samuel stands at the room's entrance and motions for me to get out of the bed. I rush over to him as he peeks down the hallway and whispers, "We ain't got but a few seconds, so we'd better make it quick." He pulls the key ring from his pants pocket, hands it to me, and says, "I'm going to cause a distraction. But as soon as I do, you run as fast as you can to your brother's room over there, unlock his handcuffs with these keys, and both of you find a back way out of the hospital. There should be a door at the end of the hallway. And don't worry about me. You just lead him straight to the nearest woods, hide out till the coast is clear, and meet me back at the truck as soon as you can."

Without even giving me the opportunity to discuss or further study the plan, Samuel runs over to the wall nearest the nurses' station, pulls the fire alarm, grabs a stack of papers, a chair, and a few other items from the desk, slings them down the hallway, and takes off running. The two deputies abandon Cecil's door and take off running after him. Samuel darts past me with the deputies no more than ten feet behind him. A man wearing a white lab coat and a stethoscope exits the elevator and steps into the hallway right in front of Samuel, who collides with the man and knocks him to the ground. Samuel recovers quickly and takes off running again, but in a matter of seconds, the two officers close in enough that they can dive onto Samuel and wrestle him to the ground. He rolls around on the ground and giggles as if he's on the losing end of a tickle fight.

With the doorway left unguarded, I run in and find Cecil lying handcuffed to the bed. He looks at me with confusion. I guess he doesn't recognize me in my new wig. "Who are you?" he asks.

I run over and unlock the handcuffs. "It's me," I say. "Let's get out of here."

"No way. You have got to be kidding me! Is that really you, Greenway?"

The look on his face is priceless. I don't think I have ever seen him so surprised about anything. I spit out the plastic teeth into my hand. "Yes, it's me. We need to hurry. We have just a few seconds to get out of here before they figure out what's going on."

Cecil looks up at me and beams with pride, as I grab his wrist and help him off the bed. With the fire alarm still blaring and everyone still occupied by the wrestling match taking place in the hallway, I lead Cecil (encountering no resistance) out the back door of the hospital. We help each other over the fence, sprint maybe a hundred yards through the woods, and climb all the way to the top of a mountain that sits behind the hospital.

We stop for a moment to catch our breath. And Cecil notices the candy stain on my leg and assumes it's a bruise, but before he even gives me the opportunity to explain myself, he leans over and shows me the stitched-up gash on the top of his head. I think I can count seventeen stitches.

"That hurt like crazy," he says. "And it's a wonder they didn't kill me. But there I was, in the hospital bed, right after they had stitched me up, and I was feeling pretty depressed about it all. I thought for a minute that maybe I would have been better off if they had just killed me. But then there comes you busting in my room, all redheaded and bucktoothed, just to bust me out." He pauses to laugh, appearing to admire my cartoon-eagle T-shirt. "I just can't believe it; there ain't no possible way you just did that."

"I can't believe it, either," I say. "And I can't believe it worked."

With Cecil humbled in appreciation like never before, I explain to him how Stinky Joe from back home is really Samuel, and that he came all the way down here just for us and that he deserves full credit for the rescue. I tell Cecil all about how Samuel rolled me off that giant cliff, and how he had plans to put us in that hidden compartment in his truck bed to sneak us back home. Cecil's eyes get moist when I tell him that Mom and Auntie Rose came crying for Samuel to come and get us, but the moisture quickly evaporates and the laughter returns when I tell him about Samuel's freckled albino mountain man disguise and how he charged through the hospital and pulled the fire alarm and slung stuff down the hallway to get the cops to run after him.

"Samuel needs to have his head examined," Cecil quips.

"That's exactly what I told him."

"If his disguise was as bad as yours, it's a wonder that they didn't catch on to you. Nobody goes out in public looking like you're looking—orange shorts and a red belly shirt—what in the world was he thinking?"

"I don't have a clue," I say, "but it worked. I thought for sure that when we charged into the hospital looking like that, they would know something wasn't right, and I was so scared my heart started pounding away, but like I said, it worked. He might need his head examined, but he is smart, I have to say."

"I reckon so, Greenway. But I wonder if they captured him?"

"The cops had him tackled, so, maybe. But like I told you, he is pretty smart. He managed to get me free when I had twenty gunslingers aiming at me—freed me right under their noses by rolling me off that cliff."

Cecil looks at me and grins. He shakes his head and says, "But what are we supposed to do now? How is he going to get us home when he is down there, and we are up here?"

"The last thing he told me was to cut you free and run to the nearest woods and hide out until it's all clear and then meet him back at his pickup truck."

"Well, where is his truck?"

"You're going to love this," I say. "His truck is back at the sheriff's office."

"At the sheriff's office? What in the world are you talking about?"

"That's where it is. It's right there at the edge of the woods, right by the parking lot."

"Like I said, he needs to have his head examined," Cecil gripes. "That's the last place we need to be, and there ain't no way I'm going anywhere near that place."

"But we have to. He came all the way down here just to get us, and that's the only way we're going to get out of here without anybody seeing us."

"Well, I guess you're right," Cecil concedes. "But I'm not going anywhere near that place, at least until it gets dark."

I glance down at my watch and say, "We got a few hours left before it gets dark, so it looks like we'll be hanging out here for a while. I don't think there is anybody at the sheriff's office because they're all out looking for us. But I guess you're right. It will still be safer to wait until dark."

Cecil nods in agreement and reclines against a tree as I continue. "But what did they say to you back at the hospital about the girls?"

"Well, those big dummies came in there when I was chained to the bed and were questioning me about it and wanted to know where we hid the bodies. And I told them they were crazy—told them that we didn't do anything to the girls. But they said I was a liar and that there wasn't no way of talking myself out of it. They said they had all the evidence they needed, said we'd be behind bars for the rest of our lives, said that we might even get the death penalty."

"What evidence?"

"That's what I asked them, and all they could say was that they found Janie's purse and Cass's jacket with some blood on it. They tried to say that we came to church the morning after they went missing and we had a terrible look on our faces like we had done something wrong. I told them that if I had a bad look on my face, it was because they stood us up that morning when they'd promised us breakfast. But that is all they said—couldn't tell me anything else."

I lie back on the ground beside Cecil and stare into the sky through the treetops, waiting for it to get dark and wondering what will ever come of all this. I just hope that Samuel didn't get captured and is waiting for us at his truck, because I don't know what we are going to do if he's not.

23

For the next few hours, Cecil and I ponder and discuss all the things that have happened since we arrived in Griggs Town. And almost every morsel of conversation that takes place on this mountain seems to be filled with the deepest and darkest forms of hopelessness known to man. No matter how many times we go over random hypothetical situations, we can't seem to rationalize how we ended up being sought for the murder of Cass and Janie. This whole predicament has Cecil and me so emotionally confused that we don't know whether to fear for our murderous label or mourn the loss of the two girls who almost stole our hearts. But we seem to bounce back and forth between the two terrible emotions.

And as the sun begins to set, we figure that it's close enough to dark to start heading toward Samuel's pickup truck. Rather than descending back down the mountain and trying to sneak through town, we decide it is safer for us to stay on the mountain and walk the ridgeline as far as we can. After a few minutes of walking, we reach a section where the ridgeline we're following merges with three other ridgelines.

To our left are two deep valleys with a steep ridgeline between them; to our right are two more deep valleys with another steep ridgeline between them. And in front of us sits a third steep ridgeline that sits high above the other valleys. It is a confusing place, and we're not sure which ridgeline or valley might take us closer to Samuel's truck, but we decide to try the ridgeline that sits to our right first.

"Wait a minute," Cecil orders, stopping at the ridgeline's entrance, grabbing his light-blue shirt by the neck hole with both hands and pulling and ripping it all the way down the center of his chest. He removes the torn shirt from his arms, rips it in two, and tosses one of the pieces to me. "Here you go. Take this and tear it into as many strips as possible. We can take these strips and tie them around a tree every so often, and if this mountain doesn't get us where we need to be, we will at least be able to find our way back here to try one of the other mountains. There are mountains everywhere, and I am afraid we are going to wind up getting lost if we're not careful."

"That sounds like a smart idea to me," I say.

We rip up the armpit-scented fabric, and Cecil ties the first strip at the ridgeline's entrance. We take off walking, tying a strip of fabric every so often on a tree, making sure that whenever we tie a new piece of fabric, it is within sight of the last piece of fabric we tied. And every time we stop to tie a new piece of fabric, we take a minute to scrutinize the landscape of the valleys below, but nothing looks familiar.

We continue walking until the steep ridgeline we are on declines and leads us to the bottom of a bowl-shaped valley at the base of another mountain. We stop to tie a strip of the light-blue fabric on a tree and listen, hoping that the faint sound of someone talking or a dog barking will show us the direction of town. But the only sounds that fill the sky are the sounds of birds. There is no sign of town.

The last light of the setting sun slips behind the trees above us, casting an eerie shadow of crooked tree branches on the forest floor. In a matter of seconds, the shadow grows wider and taller until all the remaining slivers of sunlight are shut out. With just the moonlight on our side, we scramble to locate a strip of the blue fabric tied on a tree to assure us that we can find our way back. Fortunately, Cecil manages to find one. We gather around the marked tree and look for the next piece of fabric, spinning with urgency and scouring the dim valley for another, but we cannot make sight of anything. We give it another try. Another spin. Another scour. Still nothing. And if that isn't disheartening enough, we manage to lose sight of the last marked tree.

This feeling of familiarity that I desperately long for evades me, as every direction I turn looks the same as the last. It's just one silhouette of a tree after another and no light-blue fabric around a tree.

An array of impossible questions seizes my thoughts. Where are we? Which way out of here? What are we going to do now? I hate desperate questions that I don't know the answers to. The only thing that I know is that we are lost. I've been misplaced many times, but I've never been lost like this before. It's a wretched feeling to be standing on one small, square patch of earth and not knowing which way is left, right, forward, or reverse. After all we've been through since we arrived in Griggs Town, being lost should be considered only a minor inconvenience, but this helpless feeling I have seems to suggest that being lost feels just as lousy as everything else.

We panic and take off running through the darkness. Cecil and I take turns leading each other. We have no idea where we are going or what we are doing. We are just running. We reach a mountain, unsure if this is the mountain we descended earlier or not, but we charge up the mountain as fast as we can, tripping over branches and other bits of woody debris. We get to the top of the mountain and stop.

Cecil turns to me in the moonlight with his silhouette of a face and says, "This ain't good. I can't take this anymore. It has been one thing right after another since the moment we left Colby Valley. I cannot stand this place. Coming here has been the worst decision that I've ever made in my life. Dad and Tibbs were right for trying to discourage us from leaving Colby Valley. Everybody was right."

I take a few slow, deep breaths, trying to release these feelings of anxiety, and it seems to help some. "I know what you mean," I say. "But we're going to have to try to put our nerves on hold and stop letting them lead us around. Because if we don't get ourselves together and calm down, we will never make it out of these woods alive. We have already let our nerves get us as lost as any man could ever be."

"I don't know how you think that being calm is going to help us in the shape we're in," Cecil whines. "All I know is that I don't want to wind up being a pile of bones that somebody finds lying in the woods a hundred years from now. You know, Mom and them will never know what happened to us, and they'll be crying and wondering about us for the rest of their lives. I don't want that to happen. What are we supposed to do?"

"I don't know," I say. "All I know to do is pray, pick a direction, and start walking. I don't see any other choice, do you?"

"All right," Cecil agrees. "But let's do something and do it soon. This lost feeling doesn't feel so good."

"Okay, Cecil, follow me, and we'll try to make our way out of here."

"But I thought you were gonna pray?"

"I already did. Now follow me."

I try to ignore the terrible feeling that clouds my thinking as I lead Cecil to the highest point of the ridge. I see a faint strip of the sun's afterglow on a mountain peak in the distance, and I start thinking about how its position in the sky might help guide us. It's difficult to think clearly when your nerves are on edge, but I can almost recall the sun setting somewhere behind the silver mine on the evening that we spent sitting by the reservoir with Cass and Janie.

I don't have a clue if the sun sets in the same position in the sky every day, but if it does, getting out of here should be as easy as making sure we travel somewhere in the general direction of the sun's afterglow. I explain my idea about the sun to Cecil, and although he doesn't seem to be as open-minded about the whole idea as I am, he agrees to it. He admits that any idea is better than no idea. So, we position ourselves in the direction of the afterglow and take off walking.

In a matter of a few minutes, the afterglow fades, and for the next hour or so, we skip along several ridgelines, trying to be mindful of the direction in which the sun had set, but unsure if we have managed to maintain the correct direction. After reaching the point of exhaustion, we stop to rest and wait for morning light.

The following morning, I wake and find my eyes scanning across the flattest stretch of land I've seen since I left Colby Valley. While excited over the unexpected change of scenery, I nudge Cecil to wake him. "Look down the hill, Cecil. It looks like a cattle pasture. I think we're back in civilization again."

Cecil rolls over, gazes down the mountain, and studies the terrain. "I never thought I'd be so thrilled to wake up to the sight of a cow field," he manages to say while yawning the whole time.

He stretches. "I wonder whose field it is or what town it's in. It doesn't look like Griggs Town, does it? It's too flat, ain't it?"

"I don't know. But as much as we traveled yesterday, we might be miles from Griggs Town. We're probably in the next town over."

We take off down the mountain, climb over a low wire fence stretched along and fastened to irregular locust posts at the base of the mountain, and set foot on the edge of the field.

"Ain't no doubt it's a cow field," Cecil says. "But it's an abandoned one. Judging by how overgrown it is, there haven't been any cows here for a couple of years. It looks right much like the fields back in Colby Valley." He reaches over and pinches off a handful of grass, then sniffs it. "It's also got the same kind of grass as Colby Valley. I know it don't seem possible that we're back in Colby Valley, but I think we are."

"Grass is grass," I say. "And it's not possible that we're back home. It's just not possible. Colby Valley is, like, seventy miles from Griggs Town, and there is no way we could've gone that far."

"Well, maybe it's seventy miles by road, but that doesn't mean it can't be ten times shorter by walking the ridges like we've been doing."

"And you think that we somehow lucked out and walked straight to Colby Valley, even though we've been walking without a clue as to where we were going all night?"

"Yes. That's exactly what I'm thinking," Cecil says. "As I recall, when we got lost, you said something about you were going to pray. So maybe God got tired of hearing you whine and sent us on back home to Colby Valley."

"God never gets tired of hearing us pray. So, let's see where we are. There isn't any point in standing around here and talking about it."

24

We walk a few hundred yards and see a grand old farmhouse. It's elevated and sitting high on a foundation of crumbling cement and stone, all alone with no other bits of structure, barns, or anything else within sight. A steep roof, layered with wide and peeling strips of rusty metal, covers the top floor of the sun-faded and gray structure, while rusted sheets of metal cover the roof of the long porch that stretches across the front of the house. The entire structure, including the front porch, leans without purpose. And even though we shouldn't consider going anywhere near it, we make the decision to head up the crumbling front steps and step onto the long front porch.

We open the front door, which probably hasn't been opened in decades. We enter and search around on the ground floor, hoping to find clues about where we are. Most of the flooring consists of loose planks that are cracked and deteriorated, forcing us to be mindful of where we walk and to distribute our weight only on the underlying floor joists.

After navigating the lower parts of the house, we manage to find a few old envelopes and a postcard with a Griggs Town address on it. Because of this, we conclude that we didn't travel as far from Griggs Town as we first thought and realize we must have been running in circles when we were lost the night before. Feeling satisfied that I've seen all that I need to see, I head toward the front door.

"Where are you going?" Cecil asks.

"I'm leaving."

"Without going upstairs?"

"Why would I want to go upstairs? There's barely enough floor to walk on down here, so I know I'm not going up there."

"Oh, come on," Cecil says. "Let's just check it out really quick."

"What for? We're not doing anything here but wasting time. We need to get out of here and see if we can find Samuel. I'm sure he's still waiting on us."

"We will. But let's just check it out. It won't take us but a second. I'll walk in front and try the floor out ahead of you. We might find something we could use up there."

"Like what? About the only thing I could use is something to eat and drink."

"Well, I don't know. But if nothing else, we can at least take a look out one of the upstairs windows and see if there are any signs of town, and that might save us a ton of walking."

"All right, you go and head on up there and take a look. I'll be down here on stable ground, waiting on you."

"Okay, you big chicken, I'll go it alone," he says, pushing his shoulders back and trying to look all tough.

He places his foot on the first step of the staircase, and I hear a loud pop beneath his foot. I figure that will be enough to have him second-guessing his decision about going upstairs, but he keeps moving. The wooden treads beneath him sing with snaps and squeaks as he climbs. He gets halfway up the staircase, grabs the handrail, and turns around. "Not bad," he says. "These steps are about as stable as any—loud, but stable."

He turns back around and takes another step, this time using the handrail to pull himself up. After the next two steps, the handrail rips loose from the post and the balusters and tumbles to the ground. I cringe, expecting a chain reaction to follow. But he turns around again, surprisingly calm, and says, "Well, that was close."

I stand speechless, expecting him to admit the hazards of continuing up the flight of steps, but he turns back around and keeps stepping. "Come on," I say. "The last thing we need, on top of everything else, is for you to break a leg or something. I don't want to have to carry you out of here."

"I promise, you won't be carrying me out of here. I'm almost there. And these steps are fine; handrail's got nothing to do with 'em. Just listen—they ain't creaking as much without the handrail." I cringe again, as he drops any sense of caution and takes off running up the remaining four or five steps. He stops when he reaches the top of the stairs, turns, and proudly says, "See? I told you they were stable."

He turns around again and disappears behind a plastered wall that meets the landing, while cracks and squeaks continue as he walks away. And after a few seconds, he reappears at the landing. "Come on, Greenway," he says. "You're not going to believe this. Come up here. You have got to see this."

"I told you, I'm not going."

"But you have got to see this. Don't worry, the floor is solid up here." He jumps up and down a few times on the landing. "See?"

"Come on, Cecil. We just need to get out of here and stop wasting time."

"We will, you just got to see this first. I ain't going anywhere until you do."

"Just tell me what it is or bring it here so I can see it, if it's that important."

"I ain't touching it, and I ain't telling. Just come on."

Seeing that this will be the only way to put an end to all this, I ignore the feeling in the pit of my stomach that tells me not to go, and I make my way up the flight of ancient stairs. I turn the corner, expecting to see something miraculous, but Cecil merely points to a gray pile of something on the floor. "Look," he says. "And tell me that ain't the craziest thing you've ever seen in your life."

"And what is that supposed to be?" I ask.

"Look closer, Greenway. It's a big ol' mummified cow turd."

"You wanted me to come up here to see that?"

"Yeah," Cecil says. "Don't you see anything funny about that?"

I kneel down and study the pile. "Nope," I say. "Looks like regular cow poop to me."

"Yeah, whatever, Greenway. Use your brain. My point is, how in the world do you reckon a cow turd got all the way up here on the second floor of this rickety old house? That's because a big ol' heifer made his way all the way up the steps and was just hanging around upstairs of somebody's house and pooping."

"I guess I overlooked that," I say, "but it is strange, to say the least. I wonder what made it climb up the steps in the first place. I didn't know cows could climb steps."

The sound of a vehicle's engine distracts us from marveling over the cow poop. The engine stops and the sound of somebody slamming a car door follows. Cecil and I stare each other down with worry over who it might be. Cecil motions me to keep quiet, as if I wasn't being quiet already. "Shush," Cecil whispers, pressing his finger against his lips. "If we are quiet, they won't know we're here, and maybe they will go away."

I hope to hear them start the engine back up and drive away, but instead I am forced to hear them walking around below us on the ground floor. A nervous feeling engulfs me, as I begin to imagine who it could be. *Is it the sheriff? Is it a bounty hunter? Who is it?* I wonder. Minutes later, the familiar loud pop of the first step echoes throughout the stairwell.

Whoever it is appears to now be coming up the steps. I look around and consider all the possible avenues of escape, only to realize that the glassless second-story window that shares the same room with the cow patty offers the only getaway. Cecil notices me eyeing the window, and he extends his arm in front of me, shakes his head no, and beckons me to wait.

A choir of cracks and squeaks sing beneath the stranger's feet as he climbs the stairs, and then the stairwell falls silent. Perhaps the stranger is frightened over the condition of the steps and is considering turning around. I wait to hear what he will do next, still eyeing the second-story window, but I hear no new noises coming from the stairwell.

As the silence deepens, I begin to feel at ease, but then a man appears from around the corner and stands facing us—an older man, mid to late seventies, wearing a white button-up shirt with shiny silver snap buttons and denim bib overalls. I consider running but his smile is big, and his hands are weaponless. He breaks the silence by clearing his throat, and he says, "Let me guess . . . you came all the way up here to see the cow patty, didn't ya?"

Cecil and I stare at each other, not knowing how to answer the strange question. So, the old man continues. "Well, didn't ya? People come from all over just to see it."

Figuring that it might help us avoid any trouble, I decide to go along with it. "Yes, sir," I say. "That's why I came up the steps."

"And I'll bet you didn't know cows could climb, did you?"

"Well, as a matter of fact, I never would have guessed," I say. "And I still can't figure how he managed to get up those rickety steps without falling through them."

The old man grins from ear to ear, "That's what everybody says. And I'll bet you're wondering how the cow got back down, aren't you?"

Cecil joins the strange conversation. "I expect that he got down the same way that he got up—by taking the steps."

"No, sir," the old man says. "Cows can climb up, but they can't climb back down. Their knees aren't made for it, and they're afraid."

"Well, how'd he get down, then?" Cecil asks, continuing to eye me down, clearly sharing my confusion over the purpose of this conversation.

"He jumped," the old man explains. "Come over here and I'll show you." The man leads us over to the glassless window. "If you look down, you can still see his bones," he says. As invited, and compelled by curiosity, Cecil and I share the same window and scan the ground below us but see nothing.

We turn back to face the old man and find him holding a pistol in each hand, one aimed at Cecil, the other at me. "Don't you move," the man orders in a relaxed voice. "Just get on the ground, face down." With no choice, we do as the old man instructs and lie face down in a thick layer of dust. The man continues. "So there I was, sitting on the front porch, worrying about them taking my farm over all the medical bills, and wouldn't you know, a bunch of racket coming from the house my granddaddy built was about to bring me a million bucks. I guess my granddaddy was watching out for me."

"We're innocent. We didn't do anything," Cecil charges, his voice lifting a layer of dust from the floor and making a small cloud around his head.

"That isn't for me to decide," the old man says. "Both of you put your hands behind your backs."

As commanded, we put our hands behind our backs. He kneels down, tapes our hands together, and says, "If you're innocent, why is it that you're running? I sure wouldn't run if I was innocent."

"Listen," Cecil says, further stirring the dust on the floor. "It's more complicated than that. But we are innocent. We didn't kill those girls. That's the most horrible thing that anyone could ever do, and we wouldn't even think about it."

"Welp, if you're as innocent as you say, then I suppose you won't give me any trouble taking you in. But it seems that I read a few stories in the newspaper about you two running when you had the chance to turn yourselves in. And I also heard the other day one of you was captured, but you broke out and ran some more. Now, if you were innocent, why did you break out? That don't sound too innocent to me."

Cecil growls under his breath, and I start to worry about what he might say, but he seems to hold himself together. "It's hard to explain, but can we please just sit up and talk, so I can get my face out of the dirt?" Cecil begs. "You're the man with the gun, and our hands are tied, so we're not going to cause any trouble."

"All right, but sit up slowly," he says. "No quick moves."

We sit up to face the man, and Cecil says, "As I was saying, the reason we ran and escaped and all that is because they've done nothing but threaten us with death and imprisonment the whole time. I tried to clear our name when they had me captured, but they didn't believe me."

Cecil pauses to tilt his head forward and show the old man the gash in his head. "You see what they did to me? I was lying there sleeping, and they came over and wacked me on the head.

They could have killed me. They are all nuts, I'm telling ya. And we didn't even do anything."

"I don't know how much of what you say I ought to believe, either," the old man says, lip and jowls trembling with age. But based on the smell of things, it might be the booze that is causing him to tremble. It's hard to tell. But he says, "Now, get to your feet and head toward the stairs."

25

We follow the old man's command to stand up and head for the stairs, which he motions for us to descend. As we climb down the rickety steps, I glance behind us to see him following closely, gripping his pistols in his thin and veiny aged hands. He directs us out the front door and into the cab of his faded red and half-rusted '70s model pickup truck. I sit in the middle of the wide bench seat, and Cecil sits near the passenger window. As soon as the old man gets in and slams the door, he pumps the gas and cranks the engine. The engine roars loudly at first and then comes to a rough idle that vibrates the truck.

"It's not going to be easy to drive and keep my pistols aimed at the same time," he says. "So, if I set my guns aside, I won't be getting any trouble from you, will I?"

"No, sir," I say.

"If you want, I can hold them for you," Cecil says.

The man turns and looks at Cecil, laughs, and shakes his head but doesn't speak. He drops the pistols between his legs, yanks the shifter on the steering wheel column, and pokes away across the bumpy field.

Then, reaching under the seat, the old man pulls out a bottle of liquor, and takes a big swig of the dark brown liquid. "You know what?" he says. "When I heard all that racket in the old house, I never figured I'd find the two most dangerous men in Griggs Town, with no weapons, just a loafing in there, and eyeing a cow patty. It beats all I've ever seen, and I've been around for a few years. But what strikes me the most is that y'all just stood there when I came up them steps. All you have been doing is running, but how come you two didn't run then?"

"Well, I thought about it," I say. "But you threw me off when you came in there smiling all big and talking about the cow poop. I didn't think you knew who we were . . . but you got us good on that one."

"Yeah, I knew who you were the moment I laid eyes on you. They got your faces plastered on the front page of every newspaper. And when I saw you two in there, I figured it best to act like I didn't know who you were." His gentle elderly voice is now beginning to deteriorate into more of a drunken slur. And all I can think is that if he keeps this up, he will end up getting arrested along with us when he goes to escort us into the sheriff's office.

"Well, you sure had us fooled," Cecil says. "You were acting like folks come from all over just to see that cow turd—like it was some kind of a tourist attraction."

The old man cackles, adjusts the position of the pistols between his legs, takes another swig of the dark brown fluid, and continues poking across the bumpy field. "Yeah, well, I sure tried my best," he says. "I knew I had to take you off guard somehow, and the first thing that came to mind was that cow patty. But I have to admit, when y'all started going along with the whole yarn, I couldn't believe it. I kept thinking that I was going to start laughing and blow my whole cover. Especially when I told you he jumped out of the window, and you two goofballs went over to the window to see his bones."

The old man erupts with laughter, pauses to take another swig of the dark brown fluid, and laughs again, but this time he laughs hard enough that a nasty snot bubble emerges from his nose. He stops the truck for a few seconds to blow his nose on a handkerchief, and he taps the gas pedal again to continue across the field.

He strikes my curiosity so badly that for a moment, I almost forget that I'm on my way to be arrested. "Sir, but where did the cow go?" I ask. "And how did he get down? And now that I'm thinking about it, what kept him from falling all the way through the floor?"

"You wouldn't believe me if I told you," the old man says, now heavily slurring from all the booze.

"Sure I would," I say. "What did he do?"

But before the old man can even answer, his neck and back fall limp, and his wrinkled forehead bounces off the steering wheel and falls into my lap. "Holy moly," Cecil blurts. "The old man just passed out—and we're still rolling. Pull his foot off the gas and stop this thing!"

With my hands still bound behind my back, I manage to use my left foot to kick his foot off the accelerator. The truck rolls for a few more feet and stalls in the middle of the field.

I sit still with the man's limp body weighing on me as Cecil manipulates the door handle with his foot until he can kick open the door. He exits the truck, uses the edge of the open truck door to cut the tape from his hands, and runs around to the driver's side door to open it. He pulls at the man's shirt enough to lift him off me. I slide away from the man, as Cecil releases his shirt and lowers his upper body into a lying position on the seat of the truck cab. I exit the truck, disgusted at the sight of the man's pale face resting atop a bundled mess of seat belt straps and buckles. Using the edge of the truck door, I manage to cut the tape from my hands the same way Cecil did.

As I stare at the man, a terrible feeling washes over me. "Uh, Cecil, I think he's dead," I say.

"Nah, he ain't dead. He just passed out," Cecil says.

"No, I think he's dead. His chest isn't moving. He's not even breathing."

"Don't be stupid," Cecil says. "He's passed out drunk. He has swallowed enough liquor to knock out an elephant. Just give him a few minutes, and he'll be fine."

I pass my hand over the old man's face to feel for a force of air leaving his open mouth and nose, but I can't feel the slightest breeze. "He isn't breathing," I say. "I'm telling you, not his chest or anything is moving."

"Calm down, Greenway. You don't check like that. You have to feel for a pulse or a heartbeat or something." Cecil lays two fingers on the inside of the old man's wrinkled wrist. "I can't feel anything but bones," Cecil grunts. "See if you can feel his heart and check if it's beating."

"I'm not touching him," I say. "The old man is dead. I'm telling you, he's dead."

"Good grief. I don't know what you're so afraid of. I'll do it," Cecil says.

Cecil grabs the steering wheel, pulls himself up in the truck, parks his knees in the available seat space, and reaches for the old man's chest. But before Cecil's hand even brushes the fabric of his shirt, he thrusts himself backward and launches himself out of the truck. "What is going on?" he yipes, bending over to investigate the wet spot on his pants. "The stupid seat's wet, and now my pants are wet. He done gone and peed all over himself!" He panics, kicking off his shoes and his pants.

I shut the door and move around to the driver's side. "Are you convinced now?" I ask.

"Convinced about what?" he cries. "The only thing that I am convinced about is that a drunk old man just peed on me, and now his pee has done soaked through my skin and is probably on its way to my bloodstream by now."

"Are you convinced that he's dead?" I ask. "That is what I have been trying to tell you; people empty their bladders when they die."

Cecil stretches his eyes open, and his face turns pale. He gasps and cups his face in his hands as if he is about to lose his mind. He raises his voice to a near yell. "That's just great. As if being shot at and chased and beaten over the head wasn't enough—now this! Now I'm standing here in the middle of a field, wearing nothing but my underwear, and covered in a dead man's pee."

"Please calm down for a second," I plead. "There is a house over there, and if you keep hollering like that somebody is going to hear us, and we are going to have even more trouble. They are going to think that we killed him and then try to pin another death on us."

Cecil lowers his voice, but not much. "You try calming down when you are soaked in a dead man's pee."

"I know, Cecil. I would be freaking out, too. But we cannot be standing here like this and arguing. We need to get out of here before somebody sees us."

"And go where? And what are we supposed to do with the dead man?"

"I don't know, but I suppose we'll have to leave him here. The man is dead, and it's not like we can do anything about it. But we need to go and find Samuel so he can get us back home. And in the meantime, we can try to figure out a way to let somebody know about the dead man."

"Well, I cannot be running around in nothing but my underwear, and I sure ain't putting those wet pants back on. What am I supposed to do about that?"

"Take a look behind the truck seat. It looks like there is a sleeve from a jacket or something poking out, and there might be something else there that you could wear. At the very least, there might be something you can wrap around yourself to cover you up."

Cecil climbs back into the truck, but this time he avoids touching the seat altogether. He reaches behind the seat and digs around. He pulls out a soiled wad of denim and slings it into the field. He exits the truck, sighs, and grabs the wad of denim from the ground. He shakes it until it unravels, revealing the nastiest and greasiest pair of bib overalls I have ever seen.

"They are soiled with grease and smell a little bit like a wet dog, but at least they're not soaked in pee," he says.

A deep sense of urgency starts to boil in the pit of my stomach, and I begin to feel anxious about us standing out here in the middle of the field. "Please hurry," I say. "I think we're pressing our luck by being here."

"Hold on a second. I ain't putting these overalls on without first washing his pee off my legs." He reaches into the truck and grabs the old man's bottle and starts dumping the contents on his legs, and the strong smell of liquor fills the air. And before the last drop of dark-brown fluid rolls off Cecil's legs and falls to the ground, I catch something moving out of the corner of my eye. I turn to see what it is, and I am struck with terror. It is the old man, and he is not dead. He is reaching for the steering wheel and trying to pull himself up.

I look at Cecil, but he is still distracted, caring for his legs. Afraid to even speak, I reach over and wave my hand in front of his face to get his attention. And before I can even drop my hand, a drunken slur echoes from within the cab of the truck. "Where are you boys going?"

Cecil looks at me with the exact sense of terror that I imagine is radiating from my own face. Without saying a word, he reaches down and picks up his shoes and the filthy overalls. I can only imagine what a sight we must be, with me wearing my blaze orange shorts and my red eagle belly shirt and Cecil wearing nothing but a pair of white underwear, as we take off sprinting through the field. The sound of drunken slurs carries behind us as we make our way toward the edge of the woods.

Once we are out of sight of the old man, we stop to catch our breath. The old man is not in any shape to be chasing after us, so I am not too worried about us taking a break. Cecil looks over at me and laughs hysterically. "Can you believe that just happened?" he says. "I thought for a second my eyes were playing tricks on me."

"Me too. I about lost my mind when I looked over and saw him sitting up. I thought for sure he was dead, but I guess he was just dead drunk."

Cecil slides on the pair of filthy bib overalls and his shoes. "I'm just glad that he's all right. But I sure hope he doesn't mind that I borrowed his overalls and used up all his liquor. I will have to find a way to get these overalls back to him, but I think I did him a favor by dumping out all his liquor. That's the last thing he needs."

After resting for a few more minutes, we take off through the woods. We're not sure which way will lead us to Samuel, but we assume that if we head in the same direction that the old man was taking us in his truck, we should at least get closer.

The flat land begins to give way to a landscape consisting of deep valleys and steep mountains. We climb the first mountain that we see and walk the ridgeline, observing the valley below and hoping to see something familiar. We merge with another mountain covered with deep vegetation that has jagged stone ledges poking out from the side of it, hundreds of feet above the valley below. We agree that this looks familiar, but we cannot decide why. We get to an opening in the vegetation and walk out on one of the stone ledges to investigate the scenery. From where we are standing, we can see for miles but cannot make any sense of it.

I hear what sounds like a man shouting from somewhere in the woods. Cecil looks at me, puzzled. "Do you hear that, Greenway?"

"Yeah, somebody was shouting. And it sounded like it came from somewhere to the left of us."

"You don't think it could be that drunk old man looking for us, do you?"

"There ain't no way. He was too drunk to walk, and there is no way he hiked all the way up here."

We pause to listen. A few minutes pass, and we hear no more shouting. But then a few more minutes pass, and we hear a scream.

"Yeah, there is definitely somebody over there," Cecil says. "And it sounds like they could be hurt, and they might need our help. Let's go see what's going on."

We creep through the trees in the direction of the scream. When we're partway down the side of the mountain, we see a small log and mortar structure sitting below us.

26

A faded blue tarp covers one corner of the structure's roof. Only a few old car tires and strips of rotten plywood seem to be holding it in place. Various pieces of trash, such as empty beer boxes, milk jugs, and glass jars cover most of the landscape. A rusted fifty-five-gallon drum, overflowing with empty beer cans, stands beside the leaning and moss-covered back porch. It was probably a charming cabin back in its day, but the way it's looking now would make a trash dump jealous.

This looks like the kind of place we ought to pass by and forget about, but Cecil insists that we investigate the screams that led us here. We lower ourselves to the ground and slide down the leaf-covered mountain until we are pressed up against the rustic structure below a single-pane window.

"What now?" I whisper, as this nervous feeling springs up inside me and has me questioning my sanity for being here.

"I don't know, but I guess I'll peek in the window and see what's going on in there."

"But if somebody sees you, they'll be shooting at us in about ten seconds. That is about all that anyone does around here. They just shoot at you."

"Not if they don't see me," Cecil says, looking at me with crazy eyes and grinning ear to ear, apparently trying to taunt me with his bravery because he knows I'm nervous.

Cecil inches himself toward the window, and all I can think to do is pray. Under my breath I mumble, "Please, God, help us. In Jesus's name I pray."

And before Cecil can fully stretch his legs to bring his eyes to the window, the voice of a man bounces from within the log walls. Cecil stops his journey to the window and drops back down to the ground. The skin around Cecil's eyes stretches, his mouth falls open, and he mumbles, "Did you hear that? I'd recognize that voice anywhere."

"Let's just get out of here," I plead.

"Just wait a minute. Listen! Don't you recognize that voice?"

"No. Not that I know of."

"That's the idiot who gave us a ride and stole Grandpa's pocket watch and our food."

"Are you talking about S?"

"Yes, that's exactly who it is! I'll never forget his stupid voice. Not in a million years would I ever forget it."

And before I can even attempt to talk him out of it, he pushes himself back up and peeks through the window. My heart races with anxiety as he presses his face against the glass and deposits a film of moisture with his hot breath. And after a long and uncomfortable stare, he hunches back down. He looks over at me, and I anticipate that he will tell me what he has seen. But instead of speaking, his face appears to freeze: his stretched eyes don't blink, and his open mouth doesn't budge. I punch him in the arm to snap him out of it.

"What is going on?" I ask.

"Go ahead. Stand up and look in there. You need to see this for yourself. In your whole life, you're never going to believe it."

I stand up and look through the window, and I am shocked by what I see. It's Cass and Janie, and they are alive. They are sitting on the floor, back-to-back, tied together with rope. And S, with his unmistakable long and black stringy hair, has a roll of tape in his hands, and he is taping their mouths shut.

I drop back down and sit beside Cecil. He looks over at me and says, "The girls are alive. Can you believe it? We don't have to run anymore. They're our freedom if we can set them free."

As soon as those words leave Cecil's mouth, and I begin to process what all of this means, a wonderful sense of relief consumes me. It feels like every ounce of sorrow and fear and darkness that has been weighing me down for the past few days has been lifted. But at the same time, the thought of S kidnapping Cass and Janie and holding them captive like animals fills me with anger. I hope he has not hurt the girls and wonder, *Why would he ever do such a terrible thing like this to them?* It makes no sense to me.

I envision rescuing the girls in a heroic fashion. I can see myself charging through the front door of the cabin and tackling S to the floor, but Cecil interrupts my thoughts and brings me back to reality.

"I have an idea. Keep your head low and follow me," he says.

Cecil takes off crawling, encouraging me to imitate the same slow rhythm he is using to sneak around to the left side of the cabin. He stops when he meets the edge of the porch that extends across the front of the cabin, lies down on his stomach, and motions for me to get on my stomach on the right side of him. He tilts his head over and whispers in my ear, "This is what I'm thinking, and here's what you got to do. This front porch here is low to the ground on this end, but if you crawl on your belly, you can get under there—no problem."

"I suppose I can, but why?"

"You get under there, right up under those steps," he says, pointing to the three steps at the opposite end of the porch that lead from the front porch to the ground.

"Then what?"

"Well, while you're under there waiting, I'll sneak around front—through the woods, so no one sees me—and I will hide in the edge of the woods nearest the steps. And while you are under the steps and I'm over there hiding in the woods, I will sling some rocks or something at the door. Naturally, S will come out and look around the house to see what it is. And when he comes down the steps, you reach through those steps and grab him from underneath. Grab 'em by his ankles, trip him over and pull his feet and legs through the gap between the steps. And whatever you do, don't let go. But once you got ahold of him, I'll run out with a piece of lumber and take care of the rest."

Cecil reaches over me and grabs a short piece of wood from beneath the porch. The wood is splintered and worn and has bent and rusty nails protruding from one end of it. "I'll take this," he says, "and knock him upside the head with it. It won't matter if he has a gun. It'll happen so fast that he won't even know what hit him."

"Maybe that will work, but I hope he doesn't move down the steps so fast that I can't get ahold of his ankles."

"You can do it, brother. All you have to do is remember that all our lives are depending on it." He looks over at me and grins.

"But no pressure," he says with a laugh, as he motions me to take my position under the steps.

I crawl on my stomach under the front porch for about thirty feet and position myself beneath the three porch steps. I look back and watch Cecil as he lifts himself a bit higher from the ground and does a quick crawl into the woods nearest the left corner of the house. He disappears behind the vegetation, and I wait for him to reappear in the woods located at the opposite corner of the house. But several minutes pass, and I still don't see him. I know that it will take him a little while to circle around through the woods, but the waiting is no less unbearable.

But before Cecil reappears as planned, the sound of someone turning a doorknob radiates from the cabin above me. A door hinge squeaks as a door opens. And I hear the sound of a footstep on the porch boards above me, followed by another. I look up through the crack in the porch boards, and there is S, standing right above me. Holding a pistol in his right hand, he turns his head slightly, as if scanning the woods in front of the cabin. I hope that Cecil is paying attention and doesn't accidentally reappear while S is standing on the porch.

I pray that S will turn back around and return to the cabin, but instead, he turns and walks toward the direction of the steps that I am hiding under. Dust sifts through the boards above me as he walks over my head. He takes the first step down, and I scour the woods for Cecil, hoping to see him appear, gripping the ugly, splintered piece of wood, but there is no sign of him.

S takes another step and pauses. His feet are only inches from my face, and it would be so easy for me to reach out and grab his ankles as planned, but after another quick scan of the woods, there is still no sign of Cecil. So I have no choice but to let him continue, uninterrupted, down the steps.

S takes another step and then he leaves the stairs and is standing in the dirt beside me. I know that only a small portion of the stair treads obstructs his view of me, and I am afraid that he will see me lying here in my bright red shirt and my blaze orange shorts. But even if he doesn't see me, perhaps the scent emanating from my clothing will be enough for him to smell me. And even if he doesn't smell me, perhaps the thumping sound resonating from my chest will be enough for him to hear me. The odds of him finding me right now seem to be in his favor.

And as if his odds weren't already high enough, he turns and walks out in front of the porch, then stops several feet down the hill in front of me. From where he is standing, all he has to do is turn around and he will be almost eye level with me. If he turns around, there is no way he is not going to see me.

A dime-sized spider rappels down from the underside of the porch and runs across my face, but I am too worried about my current predicament to care. I search the cavity below the porch for something to conceal me, but there is nothing for me to hide behind, nothing nearby to grab and cover myself up with. I consider crawling back out and running away, but it seems impossible for me to do it without him hearing me. I'm all out of options.

I glare down the hill and watch over him as he stands there staring into the woods. I consider what I might say to him if he turns around and sees me, but I cannot think of any reasonable excuse I could offer for being here.

After a few dreadful seconds of wondering what he'll do next, I watch him shove his pistol into the waistline of his black denim pants. He pulls a can of beer from his front pants pocket and cracks it open. After a slurp from the can, he smacks his lips, makes a kissing sound, and says, "Ahh."

As S sips on the can of beer, I scan the woods again for Cecil, wondering where he is, what he is doing. I wonder what he thinks we are going to do now that his plan to capture S has failed. But before I have any more time to ponder the question, I see a portion of Cecil's face at ground level, peeking up at me through a blanket of thick weeds and sticks and other bits of forest vegetation. It appears that he has dirt or mud smeared on his face, and he is less than fifteen feet away from S. From my vantage point, it appears S's head is positioned at just the right angle to suggest that he is looking directly at Cecil. But by some strange miracle, S is not even aware of someone lurking in the weeds. Perhaps it's inattentional blindness, or perhaps he's just had a few too many beers.

I cannot help but think, however, that if this goes on much longer, S will come to his senses and notice the outline of my brother's face, a blink of an eye, or something else. I start to feel an overwhelming sense of pressure, and I think I have to do something before things get out of hand. His gun is tucked away, his back is toward me, and he is occupied with slurping his beer, so this is probably the best opportunity that I will ever have. I hope that the beer-slurping noise will mask the sound of my movement.

27

A warm sensation boils up inside me as a surge of adrenaline floods my veins and spills over into my arms and my fingers and my legs and my toes. I roll out from underneath the porch, jump to my feet, gallop down the hill, jump through the air, and plow into S with every ounce of force that is within me. The sudden impact is so hard that his body shakes in a whiplash motion, and his beer flies from his hand. I knock him to the ground, and he rolls the rest of the way down the hill to the edge of the woods.

As soon as he stops, S fumbles to pull the pistol from his pants. But before he can withdraw it, Cecil springs from the forest floor, twigs and weeds launching from his head, and charges at him with the ugly and splintered piece of wood. Just as S gets the gun out, Cecil smacks him right between the eyes. A loud thump echoes through the woods, and S's body falls limp.

Cecil looks at me with his dirt-crusted face and says, "What in the world was that, brother? I ain't never seen anything like it. You were flying off that hill like a wild man! You had the most awful look on your face that I've ever seen. And you slammed into him so hard that his head was wobbling like a car antenna! Good job, brother. I can't believe you just did that!"

Cecil grabs the pistol and slides it into the deep front pocket of his borrowed bib overalls. Even though it doesn't look like S will be moving anytime soon, we scrounge up several feet of rope and restrain his hands and feet with a few dozen loops and knots. With S no longer a threat, we rush into the cabin to rescue the girls.

The girls look at us in alarm as we approach them. Cecil unties their rope as I peel back the silver tape from their mouths. I half expect Cass and Janie to be celebrating at the sight of us, but they instead stare us down as if they are afraid. Cass says, "Who are you, and what are you doing here? And where is that maniac?"

"Don't worry," Cecil answers. "That maniac won't be bothering you two ever again; we took care of him. He's knocked out cold and tied up."

"You are here to rescue us?" Janie asks. The suspicious look on her face appears to dissolve and a tear of appreciation forms in the corner of her eye.

"Well, why else would we be here?" I say. "You act like you don't even know who we are."

Cass shoots me a confused look and says, "I've never seen you before in my life."

"It's me, Greenway. And my brother, Cecil—over here with the mud on his face. Don't you remember us? We met you at the restaurant last week. You took us around town. You helped us get a room at the inn. You cooked us breakfast. And you both were supposed to meet us Sunday morning, but you never showed up."

"Is that really you, Cecil?" Janie asks, as the pooled-up tear in the corner of her eye breaks free and runs down her cheek. She lifts herself to her feet, walks over to him, and stares him in the face. "I can't believe it. It *is* you! I didn't recognize you in those overalls or with all that mud on your face." Clearly relieved, she draws in a deep breath, kisses Cecil on his muddy cheek, and asks, "Have you been drinking?"

"Trust me, I haven't been drinking," Cecil says, "but a drunk old man passed out and sort of peed on me, and all I had to wash the pee off me with was a bottle of liquor. And that's how these nasty bib overalls came about. Because his pee ruined my only pair of pants. It's a long and crazy story, but I'll tell you all about it sometime."

Cass stands up and eases over to me. She stops a few feet in front of me and eyes me from head to toe. Her facial expressions shift back and forth a few times, between amusement and confusion, and then she stops inspecting me, stares into my eyes, and grins. She grabs my shoulders, pulls me closer to her, and clenches me in her arms. She kisses me on the cheek and pulls away. "It really is you," she says. "But what in the world are you wearing? What's with that silly belly shirt and the short shorts? And what's with that crazy red wig?"

My heart sinks a little over her last question. I reach up and feel my head, and I am dumbfounded. Samuel's wig is still on my head. *How can this be?* I've been wearing this stupid thing since yesterday and didn't even know it. I was lost in the woods in it, and I even slept in it. I rip it off my head and sling it at Cecil. It misses and flies past him. Admittedly, it is funny, but I am feeling too embarrassed to allow myself the freedom to laugh about it yet. "Cecil! Why in the world didn't you tell me that I was still wearing this stupid wig?"

He explodes with laughter, and the girls join in with their own giggles. "Sorry about that, brother," Cecil says in the most sarcastic and insincere tone. "I figured I'd let it go on for as long as I could. I started to tell you about it back when we were in the farmhouse eyeing the cow poop, but it was just too funny. Everything was funnier with the wig on. And you should have seen yourself flying off that hill and tackling S earlier, with that thing on your head. That was the most awesome thing I've ever seen in my life." Cecil and the girls share a few more rounds of laughter over the wig and even a few rounds of laughter over my short shorts and belly shirt.

There is so much laughter coming from this cabin that you would never guess we had just knocked out a kidnapper and set his captives free. You would think there would be a lot more crying at a time like this, but I guess it's always better to laugh than it is to cry.

But all the laughter is soon replaced with a series of gasps, as I explain to the girls how my ridiculous outfit came about. They are shocked to hear that everyone has been chasing us around town, shooting at us, and accusing us of murdering the two of them.

"Look at this," Cecil says, unbuttoning the strap on his bib overalls and apparently reaching into his underwear. He pulls out a piece of paper, unfolds it, and holds it out for the girls to see. "I know it's hard to believe, but look at this. Greenway's not kidding you."

I peer over Cass's shoulder to see the paper that Cecil is holding. And to my surprise, he is holding a piece of paper that reads:

WANTED

CECIL AND GREENWAY POCHAW
SUSPECTED OF MURDERING
CASS TRISTON AND JANIE WALLY
$1,000,000 REWARD

"Where did you get that?" I ask.

"Oh, I um . . ." he says, but he doesn't answer.

"No, I'm being serious. Where did you get it?"

"Okay, Greenway. You know when we were sleeping in shifts up on the mountain by the reservoir, the night after they surrounded me at the inn, the first night that we were on the run?"

"Yeah."

"Well, I was starving. I know it was wrong, but when you were sleeping that night, I snuck into town to find some food. And that's when I found the wanted poster. I was going to tell you, but I had to keep it to myself because I knew you'd be mad that I went to town that night. I'm sorry."

"Well, Cecil, in that case, I'm sorry, too."

"You're sorry for what?"

"Well, the funny thing is, I sort of did the same thing as you. But it was on the second night when we were up on that same mountain. I was hungry and tired and tried to wake you up so I could get some sleep, but you wouldn't wake up. And it made me so mad that I decided to sneak into town to get myself some food. I'll never forget it; I had raw onions from Wringley's Produce and chocolate and jelly beans from May's Sweets. But most of the jelly beans got wet in my pocket and that's how my leg got to looking like this."

Cecil and the girls marvel at my stained leg for a moment, and then they stare me down with grossed-out looks on their faces.

"Chocolate, onions, and jelly beans?" they ask.

I pause long enough to share a chuckle with them, and say, "But the only difference is that I found this piece of paper that doesn't say anything about murder." I pull out a damp piece of paper from my sock, unfold it, and show it to him:

W A N T E D

CECIL AND GREENWAY POCHAW
$1,000,000 REWARD

Cecil's mouth drops open at the sight of it. He takes a step toward me, tucks his lips, squints his eyes, and tilts his head—a look that might suggest he's about ready to punch me. "I can't believe you went into town to eat while I was sleeping," he gripes.

"Yeah. I know the feeling. Tell me about it."

He reaches over and slaps me on the back of the head. "I can't believe you risked your life for onions, chocolate, and jelly beans. That's about the nastiest combination there ever was. When I snuck into town, there were people everywhere, but at least I risked my life for something worth eating. I just went down to the bridge where the bakers throw out bread and pulled me a loaf out of the bushes." He reaches over and slaps me on the head again. "Now let's get these girls home and get our freedom back."

We lead the girls outside and find that S is still knocked out cold. The girls seem pleased to find him oozing blood from his mouth and nose. We tell the girls about our previous run-ins with S, and how he gave us a ride when we were first on our way to Griggs Town. We tell them all about the windshield wiper incident and about how he came back and stole our food, water, and our grandpa's pocket watch. But their experience with S was certainly far worse than ours.

They tell us that S kidnapped them after the last evening that they spent together with us at the reservoir. They explain to us that they were on their way home, and that he pulled up beside them in his car, pulled a gun on them, and forced them both to get into the front seat of his car.

"But why did he kidnap you? Did he hurt you?" I ask.

"No," Cass says. "He raised his hand like he was going to hit us a few times, but he never did. He just told us that he was holding us for ransom and that he would let us go as soon as he got the money. Somehow, he had learned that my daddy is the mayor and that Janie's dad is the sheriff, and so he got the idea that he could get a lot of money for us. He went out several times and tried to deliver a ransom note, but he said that there were roadblocks and cops everywhere and that he would have to try again later."

"But what is all this talk about blood?" Cecil asks. "When they had me chained to the hospital bed, they said that they had evidence that we had murdered you. They told me that they found a purse and a jacket with your blood all over them."

"That was *my* purse," Janie says. "When he made us get into that disgusting car of his, I cut my ankle on one of those meat cans that he had on the floorboard. He had a pile of cans and trash in there. But I sliced my ankle open on one of those can lids—or something—and I was bleeding terribly. I got blood all over my purse, my shoes, and everything. I was so upset. But Cass used her jacket to apply pressure on the cut until it stopped bleeding. And when he managed to get his dumb car to stop, he put a piece of tape over my cut and threw my purse and the jacket out the window. I could have killed him for that!"

While we are listening to Janie tell her story, S wakes up and looks around at everybody. He sits up, spits a stream of blood from his mouth, and says, "Ohhh, would you look at that. It's Cecil and Greenway. Which one of you hit me in the face? You broke my nose and just about made me bite off my tongue." He wiggles his hands and tries to free himself from the rope that we tied around his wrist. "You just wait until I get loose."

"It was me that hit you in the head," Cecil boasts, "and I'll do it again if you keep running your mouth. Now, where's the pocket watch that you stole from me? That was my grandpa's. He gave it to me before he died."

"I ain't got no watch. Don't know what you're talking 'bout."

Cecil kneels down and extends his hand to reach into S's pants pocket. But S starts squirming from side to side and cursing loudly. Cecil hurries back into the cabin and returns with a roll of silver tape in his hand. He kneels back down and starts the tape at the left side of S's face, runs it across his lips, lifts up his head and runs the tape behind his head and back across his lips again.

"We'll try this again," Cecil says.

The girls and I stand back and watch as Cecil reaches into each of his pockets one at a time, while S produces a muffled yell from beneath the silver tape and rocks his body from side to side but is unable to resist the search. Cecil withdraws Grandpa's pocket watch and smiles as he opens the watch and inspects it. "It's still ticking," he says. Cecil places the chain of the pocket watch around his neck like a necklace. Once he appears to be satisfied with the position of the pocket watch around his neck, he looks to the girls and says, "Which way out of here? We need to get you girls back home and get our freedom back."

Janie points down the hill and says, "We need to follow that path; it will take us to the main road."

Cecil unties the rope from S's ankles and instructs him to stand up and follow us, but he refuses. Cecil says, "I don't know about you, Greenway, but I ain't wasting my time with him. You get one of his ankles, and I'll take the other. And we'll drag his scrawny hind end out of here. I'd say that by the time we get to the bottom of the hill, we won't even have to ask him to get to his feet." I happily agree.

And with the sound of S's back scraping against the hard earth, the five of us take off down the side of the mountain. But our descent is cut short by a loud and mysterious voice.

"Hey—wait a minute!" a man's voice shouts from the mountain above us.

We drop S's feet to the ground, and Cecil hurries to pull the pistol from his front pocket and aims it up the hill. "Everybody get down," he whispers, motioning to us with a rapid downward movement of his hand. He cocks the pistol and shouts up the hill, "I have a gun, and I ain't afraid to use it!"

"Hold on—don't shoot!" the man shouts back. "It's just me, Stinky Joe. I'm on my way down."

Cecil looks over at me and grins in amazement, but he still holds the pistol steadily in his hand.

Samuel makes it down to where we are, but he's out of breath and panting by the time he reaches us. He finally says, "I saw those blaze orange shorts and that red shirt moving through the trees and knew right away who it was. Figured there couldn't be anyone else on earth wandering around in the woods in a getup like that. But it's good to see you again, Greenway. I was worried about you." He pauses to shake Cecil's hand and continues. "And it's good to see you, too, Cecil. I see that you all found the ladies that they accused you of killing. But who is this that you got tied up here?"

"That's the kidnapper," I say. "He was holding the girls captive in that cabin up the hill."

Samuel kneels down and studies S's bloody face. "Looks like you knocked him a good one. That's a broken nose if I've ever seen one. But how in the world did you manage to find the girls?"

"I don't know," I say. "All I know is that God must have led us to them. There is no other explanation. But what about you? How in the world did you manage to find us?

"Well, after getting loose from everybody at the hospital, I went back and waited for you both at my truck like we planned. But I got to worrying after I didn't see you that night, so the next morning I went out looking for you. And you know what? Turns out I was all out of disguises. So I just went out dressed as my normal self, and not a soul recognized me. But I was passing through town on my way to the woods behind the hospital to search for you, when I overheard an old man talking to some police officers. He'd pulled up in a red pickup truck and he sounded like he was as drunk as a billy goat. And he was telling the officers how he'd had you both in custody before you all escaped into the woods near his house. But when the cops asked him to describe you, he tried to tell them that one of you was a redhead and was wearing a belly shirt and short shorts, and they just laughed in his face over it and arrested him for being drunk. But I knew that was a perfect description of Greenway. So after the cops took him away, I searched his truck and found his vehicle registration with his address on it. And when I found his house, I went searching through the woods for you both. I was about ready to give up until I heard somebody cussing and hollering. And that's when I made my way down there and saw those blaze orange shorts and red T-shirt moving through the trees."

"Well, I'm happy you found us—that's a miracle in itself. But you just about missed us," I say.

"Just about, but I'm sure glad I didn't. I'm glad that I found you all and that you're okay. And, boy, am I glad that you found the ladies and they're okay. That will sure make it easy to clear your names. But what are you going to do now with all that reward money?"

"What reward money?" Cecil and I ask collectively.

"This reward money. Look here. People were going around town and handing these out." Samuel pulls out a piece of paper from his pants pocket and unfolds it. It has a picture of Cass and Janie on the front, and it reads:

MISSING

$1,000,000 REWARD

FOR INFORMATION LEADING TO THE WHEREABOUTS

OF MISSING GRIGGS TOWN RESIDENTS

CASS TRISTAN AND JANIE WALLY

The girls look at us and smile. "Well," Cass says, "It looks like you guys are buying dinner this time. Now, let's get out of here and get something to eat. I'm starving."

We take off down the mountain and, in a few minutes, we are standing at the edge of an asphalt road.

"I think I know where we're at," Cecil says. "It looks to me like we're near Griggs Mountain Tunnel."

I look to Cass and Janie for their opinion, and they nod their heads in agreement with him.

Cecil grabs hold of the ropes on S's wrist and yanks him to his feet. "See?" he says. "I told you he'd be ready to walk after we drug him around a bit."

We set off walking and, just as Cecil predicted, after turning the corner we find ourselves facing the same tunnel that I struggled to get Cecil through when we first arrived at Griggs Town. I expect a little resistance from Cecil about entering the tunnel, but to my surprise he doesn't show the least amount of fear or hesitation. Instead, he simply grabs ahold of S's ropes with one hand and Janie's hand with the other, and he takes off, leading them into the tunnel before the rest of us.

Cass grabs hold of my hand, and we follow, with Samuel walking along beside us. When I woke up this morning, I never imagined that it would be possible for things to turn around and get as good as this. This morning, I was wanted for murder and was feeling so low that I was literally eyeing a cow turd in a rundown house. But now I have a beautiful girl holding my hand, and I am on my way to gain my freedom back. And now I'm rich, apparently. We left Colby Valley with only a few dollars in our pockets, but now we'll be returning to Colby with a million. Who could have guessed? I reckon that when I get back to Colby Valley, I'm going to open up a store across the street from old Mr. Jenny's store, sell everything at cost, and put that mean old man out of business. But then again, God knows that it would be so much better for all of us if I just went ahead and forgave him.